RUPTURED

MAGGIE MAE GALLAGHER

Edited by Megan Records
Copyedits by Joyce Lamb
Cover Art & Formatting by Damonza

ISBN-13: 978-0-9914817-2-9 (ebook)

ISBN-13: 978-0-9914817-3-6 (print)

TABLE OF CONTENTS

ACKNOWLEDGEMENTS

ONCE AGAIN I have to thank my editor, the stupendous Megan Records, for helping me take this book and make it shine. To my copy editor, the fabulous Joyce Lamb, for helping me put that extra sheen on my work. To the fabulous staff at Damonza, especially Alisha for your gorgeous artwork that continues to exceed my expectations and Benjamin for the beautiful formatting job.

I need to thank Angie Fox, not only for the awesome cover quote on Anointed, but for being a wonderful mentor and friend. Your support on this journey means the world to me. I need to thank Jeffrey Leigh, retired United States Army veteran, whose insights into battle formations helped me mold some of the sequences so that I could portray them with the integrity and honor they deserve. Thank you too, for your lifetime of service to our country.

This one is for my mom. For instilling within me a such strong work ethic as set by your example, believing in me at times when no one else did, and supporting me along this wonderful journey. I love you.

CHAPTER ONE

Year 83, Day 256, 18:00 Hours, After Mutari

"BREEDER."

That word. The one thing I had attempted to escape my whole life. The dull gray walls of the Densare Council rang with impunity. I glanced around at the thirteen members, each sitting rigidly upon a stone chair that looked more like a small throne with intricately carved Celtic symbols paying tribute to a bygone era. They always reminded me of Celtic tombs.

The Densare Council ruled our world with an iron fist of justice created in the fiery destruction of the Mutari. When the Mutari hit Earth eighty-three years ago, mankind had been caught with their pants down around their knees. Drystan, Lord of Infernus, unleashed his demon armies upon the globe in a worldwide campaign to annihilate the human race. He almost succeeded.

The Densare Council, forged under an alliance of

nations, sat in confident repose encased in their long white robes, their faces devoid of any remorse at my sentence. They governed and the people obeyed their orders without question.

I was never one for minding orders.

"But … my platoon. I'm the only one qualified to lead them." Surely there were other Cantati women they could convert into Breeders. Our numbers were not that horrible. In fact, we had made a comeback from last year's dismal head count. The human population stood at more than thirty thousand by our last estimates. My expertise was needed in the field, not the bed chamber. What was the point of making a child if you could not protect him or her? Maybe if the Densare Council left the safe confines of the Compound once in a while they would see what their rulings mitigated.

"You are relieved of your command," stated Amelia, the Coven Mother. Her blond hair flowed around her face as she rubbed the bulging ball in her abdomen. Iain, the Cantati Forces' staunchest ally on the Council, nodded his balding head in agreement, toppling the other eleven from any disagreement. They all did their part for the continuation of the species. This was the Coven Mother's fourth pregnancy, and I knew she was only half a dozen years older than I. Would that be me in a few years? On my fourth pregnancy, my body no longer fit to fight? I hated them for this.

"Do I even get to choose the lucky guy?" While I was far from being a prude, I would like a little input on which man I spread my legs for. Granted, the pool to select from was relatively small, and of that tiny selection, there were but a choice few whom I would prefer.

"The Council has already made the decision for you." By the gods, of course they had. They decided everything for us mere mortals. Apparently, we were incapable of selecting our mates.

Who would they give me to? The Council had already taken away that which mattered most: my freedom. It wasn't like I could use Synaptic Pathways Diversion to wiggle my way out of this one. The Coven Mother would smell a spell from me a mile away.

"Who?" My body clenched. Please let it be Luke or Quinten. With one of those two, I would at least get some measure of freedom, and I was certain if I played my cards right, it would go much better than I hoped.

"Cade, lieutenant of Blue Squad and General O'Hare's second-in-command."

Him? Over my dead body!

That behemoth had always watched me. He was a mountain of a man, a good soldier, and sadistic with a dash of insanity on the side. He liked killing demons for sport, and not just because the Densare ordered him to. He took pleasure in it, reveled in it, and even collected trophies from his kills. I had to submit my body to that. Kill me now. I would rather face a rampaging horde of Feronte demons, fireballs and all, than submit my body to Cade's brutal ministrations.

Bloody hell, we would kill each other inside of a week.

"You may go now, Alana. You are to report to his chambers immediately." The Coven Mother tapped her gavel, my prison bars slammed around me, and all before breakfast. So our first time would be in his room above ground, and not in mine? Better to get the baby-making underway as soon as possible, before the reality settled in and women in the barracks revolted from the constraints placed upon them.

I stomped out of the chamber. It was the only way I could respond without being tossed out of the Compound for good. One did not cross the Council and live to tell the tale, unless I preferred to take my chances in the Desert. And while I detested the thought of Cade having an all-access pass to my body, no one survived long in the Desert. It was what we called the land outside The Wall. Forty years ago, the Densare had commissioned a wall ten feet thick and a hundred feet tall with a ten-mile diameter with the Compound in the center. It had been constructed as a way to bar demons from entering our living quarters. Heavily guarded and fortified, the stone-and-steel wall protected us, guarded our doorstep. Every compound worldwide had a similar barrier. It was the only thing protecting us from complete extinction.

I had become the thing I had strived to avoid. In my heart, I had known this day would eventually arrive. It's why I had cozied up to Zarek. But when he perished in a raid six months ago, I had prayed the persistent demon attacks would provide me with more time.

The tunnels of the Compound bulged with refugees. In the past week, our wall defense had been breached four times. Those living outside the Compound had retreated from their homes and were now living inside the already cramped quarters.

The Densare had expanded the tunnels in the underground labyrinth over the past eighty years. With more and more people requesting asylum within the Compound, the original building, which at one time had been called the Tower of London, had become insufficient. The walls had been expanded and reinforced to withstand demon raids. There were markers, doorways made of steel, fashioned into extra lines of defense. Should one level or area become infected, the door releases could be triggered and blown. I tapped on one set as I passed a room full of Breeders, all in varying stages of pregnancy. Some even held their bundles of joy in their arms. We must protect the future of our species.

That would be me soon. Forced to reside with

the other pregnant women and children, no longer an individual but a vessel.

No way out. Cade and the Council were not known for their patience. Synaptic Pathways Diversion or SPD was out of the question. Any incantation that might actually work would likely be too much for me to handle. My expertise was in the field fighting, not the mystical woo-woo stuff the Coven did.

Stepping onto an elevator, I returned above ground and left the Council building, crossing the Tower Green to the barracks. The cloying aroma of cow dung and onions wafted on the misty evening. We used the Green for growing vegetables and housing the few animals we were able to spare from demon slaughter.

Ancient stone housed the Cantati Forces living quarters. Sitting four stories high and six stories deep, they led to a series of underground tunnels the Densare Council had built up as a last line of defense. Guards patrolled the grounds around the clock. Demons normally preferred attacking at night, although that hardly stopped Drystan and his minions from launching deadly assaults during the day.

I entered the barracks, closing the door behind me. With each footfall toward Cade's room, my fate sealed itself. I was no longer an elite Cantati lieutenant and platoon leader, but a chattel good for nothing but birthing new Cantati into the world. The thought of bringing a child into the destruction that was mankind nauseated me. Until we fully beat back Drystan's armies once and for all, it was irresponsible of us as a species to bring children into the world. They were too innocent, too small, and too bloody soft for this world.

I remembered all too well my shipboard journey as a child with my father from Maryland. The United States no longer existed. Seventeen years ago, our country had been overrun by swarms of demons in a night raid. It was the night my mother had been gutted by a Hatha demon. Survivors fled by ships to Compounds in other countries. The vessel my father and I boarded transported us to England. This Compound had housed close to ten thousand people when we arrived. In the seventeen years since, our losses had been substantial. Today, we had one thousand, one hundred and twelve inhabitants.

Cade's quarters were located on the top floor of the barracks. It was a far cry from mine, housed five stories below ground, where it was more difficult for demons to reach. All women lived below ground, under Council law. It was an extra layer of protection. If demons infiltrated the main hub, they had floors of able-bodied men to rip to shreds before they discovered the women and children. Drystan's war on us had rendered gender equality null and void. And yes, I would experience supreme pleasure in ridding the world of that monster.

I took the stairs two at a time. At the top, I noticed

my hands shook. I wanted our initial mating over with that way I knew what to expect from him, rather than waiting for the event to occur, not that I had much say in the matter. If I had my way, I would not be submitting my body to anyone, unless I desired him.

Which I bloody well didn't.

Soldiers stood at attention and saluted as I passed. I would miss that, the respect, the order, the camaraderie of my unit. They were my family. We had very few females in our ranks, and I never minded, not the rules I had to break to ascend the ranks nor the extra hours I had spent training to become a bigger badass than the rest of them. I liked that it made me unique among the Cantati. I adored the thrill of the hunt, of going out on patrol in the dead of night with men for whom I risked my life and vice versa. A simple ruling by the Council and my world vanished. The unfairness of it, that I was being forced to lose myself for the greater good, opened a deep well of sorrow in me, one I never liked to contemplate, and it would now consume me.

By the time I reached the fourth floor, my heart fluttered in my chest. My feet felt like they had bricks strapped to them as I marched toward Cade's metal door. I did not want this man. I tasted bile at the thought of his body up against mine.

Clank, clank, clank.

My hand rapped against metal, and the invisible chains around me tightened. The door swung inward.

Cade stood there, in all his six-foot-four glory, the white army-issue T-shirt stretched across a mountain of muscles. An inky black tribal tattoo started at his left elbow and disappeared under the strained confines of his shirt. His face had been carved from stone, all sharp angles and planes, his head shaved clean of hair save for the stubble of the goatee lining his angular jaw. His nose was no longer straight from a couple of breaks and sat slightly crooked on his otherwise handsome face. His eyes were liquid pools of darkness as they assessed me.

"Come in, Alana." He said my name like a benediction. It's not like men had a ton of opportunities for sex, not with the limited numbers of available females. Would he want to start right away or would he give me time? Not that it mattered—the Council had just presented me to Cade like an offering to a god.

Saying nothing, I crossed the threshold and shivered. His room was functional at best. A full-size bed, its linens precisely made. I considered it the bed of doom. At the foot of the bed stood a standard army chest that likely held any additional clothing and personal weapons. Traces of unease skittered down my spine. I could not let him see how much this bothered me. Would he take me now? Not that the timing mattered, it would happen, whether I wanted it to or not. Any other woman would be dancing for joy at the chance to bed him; I seemed to be built incorrectly and could not force myself to accept it. It's not that I objected to him, per se, but to the idea that I was no longer in control of my own destiny. The Council had stripped me of my choices.

By the goddess, I surveyed the room further for weaponry and his trophies, of which I had now become one. I wished for my gun or one of my blades. I felt naked without them. A wooden nightstand rested near the bed and held a single lamp. To my left was a bookshelf, a door to a private bathroom, and a small table with two chairs. I wondered where he put his trophies, though that was a little bucket of crazy I did not wish to view any time soon. I had enough issues to deal with without including that freak show.

"Take a seat." He gestured to the table, which held a bottle of clear liquid, probably the rotgut moonshine some of the guys were brewing, and two glasses. The breath I had not realized I held, expelled in a rush. He wouldn't force me immediately. That was something at least. And a drink would take the edge off, even though that stuff burned a whole in your stomach. In fact, it might be better if I downed the bottle and was rendered unconscious for the festivities that were about to ensue.

I sat on the edge of the pinewood chair positioned next to the window. I had an escape route if needed. Granted, I would break both legs in the process, but it was an out, especially when I felt like a rat in a maze.

"Look, I'm not a monster, and I know this isn't what you want." He closed the door, sliding the deadbolt and locking us inside. Locking me in. I was not known for theatrics, but felt a swoon within reach. I hated enclosed spaces, and noticed my hands still shook.

"It's not that, I …" I kept my fingers from clenching. I could not show weakness or he would swallow me whole in the process. Sweat rolled down between my shoulder blades.

Bloody hell. I had to chill out. It was just sex. I did not even need to fully participate, but could let him do his business and move on. It wouldn't kill me. I might not enjoy it, but that was not the point.

He held up a hand. Pulled his chair out, turned it around and straddled it.

"But I will follow the orders of the Council. You belong to me. I won't be cruel or force you tonight. I will give you today to become familiar with me before we consummate our union. I have a mission within the hour, but will visit you tomorrow evening. I will start visiting your room each night at an arranged time depending upon my mission schedule." It didn't sound like he liked that little tidbit, that he would be forced to come to my room. Except, the Council had decreed that women were to live below ground as a means of protection. So what he wanted didn't matter. He still got to bed the General's daughter, just not on his own terms.

Although, the fact that he had given me an extra night of freedom was more than I had expected from him. Maybe I could, if not feel something for him, at least be less opposed to being with him.

"Cade, I don't mean to be difficult. I don't like that my choice was taken from me. We are both platoon leaders and used to making our own decisions, other than what General O'Hare dictates."

Could he understand my side at least? Then maybe I wouldn't feel like I was standing before a firing squad.

"I won't say I'm displeased. You are one hell of a warrior, and the offspring we will make together will be something fierce. It would help, though, if you didn't look like you'd just swallowed an explosive." He meant it. His deep voice rumbled as his gaze roamed over me, stopping ever so briefly at my chest and juncture of my thighs before returning his smoldering stare to my face. There was no way this man would allow me to lie there, unresponsive, while he did his thing. He would make me be present, would not accept any wooden responses, and would do his damnedest to make sure any walls I had built were waylaid into dust.

It sucker-punched me how much he desired me. A tiny shimmer of heat responded—no three-alarm fires, but it was something that might help me make peace with the Council's decision.

"I'm sorry. I will do my best. But …" I apologized, even though it was far out of my control.

"I'm not who you would have chosen." He grimaced, eyes boring holes into my soul. What did he see? How broken I was? That I wanted something I couldn't name, wanted it with my entire being, but had never come close to feeling it.

I opened my mouth to disagree.

"Don't deny it. Had the Council left the choice up to you, more likely than not you would have picked a lesser man you could bend to your will. I am not that man."

I felt my cheeks redden and heat flush my skin. Was I that obvious? I returned his caustic stare. His eyes missed nothing and were about as alive as stone. He was right, our children would be fearsome creatures, miniature Cades with terrible battle cries. I shuddered at the thought. I could not move past the wretched idea that my body belonged to this man.

I must be the worst sort of Cantati. I knew it seemed I cared nothing for the continuation of the human race, when that could not be further from the truth. When the Mutari hit, we did not just lose most of the world's population, we lost our ability to love. What was love compared to the human race continuing? What was love compared to the Coven's ability to select individuals who were best suited to further the Cantati powers? It was their way of genetically engineering our species and strengthening the powers of our race. Most children in our world grew up without their father's influence other than training. Mine certainly had not spent more time with me than he'd had to and did only his duty. Did he love me? Sure, but not enough to stop the ultimatums of the Council.

Bugger it, love was for children. It did not exist in the Cantati world. The lack made me question why we fought Drystan at all. There was no warmth left in this world. And what I craved, what I longed for, the stories of love I had read, were fairy tales from an age that died eighty-three years ago.

So I turned that need outward, trained harder, became the better soldier. I bled for my people, sacrificed the daylight and lived for the night, devoted my life to ending the war that almost eradicated us. I loved my job, loved everything about it and gave the Cantati all of me, save one thing. But now they wanted my soul, too.

"I'll see you tomorrow, then." I shot out of the chair like a launched grenade and made a beeline for the door. The walls shrank as my panic escalated. Trapped, I felt my pulse thump wildly. I had to escape, even for a short while. I doubted that once he deemed it time for us to begin, he would allow me to leave my prison room for more than meals.

Cade stood with me and halted my escape. Full-blown panic enveloped me, and my hands fisted defensively as he dragged me into his arms.

"To seal the Council's command."

His lips crashed over mine. This was no gentle seduction, but a full on frontal assault. Instinctively, my hands shoved at his mammoth chest. Shock froze my brain. Every fiber of my being protested the swiftness of his brutal mating. His arms squeezed air from my lungs, and I gasped. Cade pressed his advantage and penetrated my mouth with his tongue, mimicking what he was permitted to do with my body by order of the Densare Council. As his mate, even after I was pregnant, I was his now and forever until death.

He moaned as I gagged on his tongue, which he forcefully shoved far down my throat. I saw red. Without considering the ramifications, I bit down. I bit down hard, shoving all my hatred into my bite, until I drew blood.

Cade yelped and shoved me against the door, making the hinges rattle. He wiped blood from his mouth and tongue onto the collar of his white shirt, staining the fabric. My soul iced at the ferocity of his features. I had witnessed this look of his a time or two, right before he decapitated an Efrit, a nine-foot beast bred in the fires of Infernus with a head shaped like a crocodile and known for its lightning fast decapitations. How bad would his retribution be?

"Bitch. Since you like it rough, we can begin as soon as I return from my mission. Go, before I change my mind and decide to tie you to my bed and not let you up until you are with child."

He opened the door, and I stumbled out. I wiped away the tangy metallic flavor of his blood still fresh in my mouth. I felt nothing for him but revulsion. I wanted to shout at the gods. Demand that my fate belong to me instead of that behemoth.

How could I willingly submit my body to him?

CHAPTER TWO

"GENERAL, I MUST speak with you."

I marched into my father's office, uncaring of potential recourse. He was conferencing with the other Compounds: Versailles, Berlin, Kremlin, Cape Town, Sydney, Hong Kong, and Rio. The holographic images of each general were displayed on ancient analog computer monitors lining the walls. Dressed in tan fatigues, my father had gray hair buzzed so close to the scalp that the overhead fluorescent lighting gave it a ghostly sheen. He held up his hand toward me, silencing any outburst.

"General, by our latest estimates, should the attacks increase, we will be at full-scale war before the week is out," General Rémy, leader of the Versailles Compound and eldest of the commanders, commented with the barest trace of an accent. A full head of thick, stark-white hair crowned his ruddy, wrinkled features. The man had to be nearing eighty. Living that long in these times was a feat of damn near mythic proportions.

My father returned his concentration back to his audience, not allowing my interruption to interfere with his meeting. He commanded the devoted attention of every one of his men. A trailblazer among the Cantati since I was a child, he was powerfully built, even at fifty, from a lifetime spent fighting Drystan's armies. When he entered a room, men quieted. When he spoke, men listened. He had always made me proud as a child, so I knew with every fiber of my being that it was my destiny to follow in his footsteps.

"Is this true?" my father inquired, and glanced at each of his generals, hardened warriors bred in the aftermath of the Mutari, who had been elevated through hard work and circumstance. Generals tended to have very short life-spans. They had all been in their positions only half a dozen years, as much as I could remember. My father was the only one I knew of who had been in a position of command most of my life. He had survived through steely determination and men who were willing to sacrifice their lives to ensure he continued to lead us.

General Phi Gong, from Hong Kong, responded, "Yes, we are experiencing rising numbers as well. In the last week, my troops have been raided on nightly patrols by demons in larger platoons than we have witnessed in a generation."

"The Rio Compound has been attacked twice this week alone," said General Luis Borges.

Really? Only twice? We had been hit four times

this week, and you did not see us whining about it. Man needed to grow a pair. The larger numbers concerned me, though. Why increase numbers now? I sent my demon sensors into overdrive, hoping they would help me with the riddle. Every Cantati was gifted with preternatural abilities, my specialty was I had a built in demon detector and could sense them within a five mile radius.

"Our compound has been hit five times in the last nine days," countered General Langstone in Australia.

So Hong Kong, Rio, and Sydney had all experienced escalations. What was Drystan's end game? None of us knew why he had unleashed his armies upon the globe. Any squad that had been sent on a mission to uncover that secret had never returned. And why now? Why the rapid surge in attacks? There was never a time he wasn't sending his minions after us, but he'd suddenly and radically changed his strategy. It made the hairs on the back of my neck stand at attention.

"It is the Council's belief that Drystan is changing the angle of his attacks," my father said. "We need to send scouts into the Desert to find the jump points. Once we locate the portals, I want a coordinated effort to destroy them. Send a platoon with as much C-4 as your troops can muster. I want to blow those sons of bitches back to hell where they belong."

That's my dad: if you couldn't beat them by hand, toss an explosive their way and see what happens. He was one of the reasons why most of the United States was a desert wasteland. When the Easter Eve raid hit the United States, the staggering numbers of enemy invaders had left the Council no choice but to detonate a few nuclear bombs. Would it come to that at the Tower Compound? The Kremlin Compound still had access to all its codes so it wasn't completely out of the question.

Even through the holographic images, his generals stonily stood at attention as he continued. "In addition, the Council is traveling to the Versailles Compound in the morning. They plan to further investigate the massive breach issue. General Rémy?"

What?! The Council was leaving! What the bloody hell for? They had not left the safe confines of the Tower Compound in more than a decade. Tendrils of unease stroked through my sensors. How vulnerable would our Compound be without them? The Compounds had divided the Coven members up as a way to utilize their gifts to add magic to our defenses. Lately, they had decided that each Compound would house one Coven member, while the rest were sent to Versailles to work on potions. The Coven Mother's absence would create gaps in our ability to defend this place.

"Yes, sir."

"I want your divisions on high alert until the Council arrives. You are to notify my office once they are securely ensconced behind your Compound walls.

We will wait to begin our assault until then." General O'Hare's voice boomed as he responded leaving no room for disagreement. The Council had promoted him to high commander recently. It was a mantle I did not believe he wanted, but as always, he followed the Council's orders.

"Is that a good idea for the Council to travel with the increased attacks?" General Rusakov asked, trepidation clouding his voice. The Kremlin Compound had been hit viciously hard recently, harder than most. I wanted to know the same thing Rusakov did. Why would the Council leave the Compound now? What squad had been assigned to protect that many VIPs? My platoon was the best by a long shot, but I would not leave the Compound vulnerable like that, even if my father ordered me to. How were they planning to travel to Versailles?

"I agree. We cannot afford to lose them," General Adler murmured, concern etched across his sunken features. Since the majority of assaults happened at night, Cantati Forces had a severe sun deficiency. Years of living at night and getting whatever shut-eye we could during the day, had taken its toll on even the most stalwart among us.

"The Coven Mother and rest of the Council not only need to investigate the massive breach General Rémy reported," my father said, "but the Coven has notified us that it is close to perfecting its growth serum and ready to begin patient trials. The Council wants to oversee the first doses. While the timing is difficult, it is irrelevant in light of our potential ability to add more fighters to our ranks."

I wondered who the test subjects would be and whether they would have a choice in the matter. With the way the Council ruled our world, I highly doubted it.

"Agreed," General Langstone replied, followed by General Anderson, General Borges, General Gong, and General Rémy.

Out-voted, General Adler and Rusakov both conceded the point. Whatever else I thought of my father, men followed his leadership.

"I want our attacks to run like clockwork. Each explosion must happen within minutes of the first detonation. General Langstone, your attack must be timed precisely at sunrise in Sydney in two days' time. That will afford the Council members enough time to be safely entrenched behind the walls of Versailles before our attacks begin. Then the rest of the Compounds will follow within minutes of the first strike. Langstone, send the exact timing to everyone in this room. Form your battalions now and send out your finest scouts."

"Yes, sir." General Langstone nodded his agreement.

"General Borges, your attack will be the only one conducted at night. Send as many as you can without compromising the Rio Compound."

"Understood, sir."

"Send me status updates on each mission, we will

reconvene in seventy-two hours. Good hunting men, and good luck to us all." He ended the transmissions and the room dulled without the light of the holograms. My father's office was fairly utilitarian. He had a wooden desk, his one concession to history, which commandeered most of the office space. The old analog monitors sat on tables that lined each wall, except the one behind him, which was lined with silver gunmetal to help reinforce the wall. A Cantati genius had discovered a way to use the old phone lines to establish connections with the other compounds.

"Why aren't you and Cade in your room?" he questioned from behind the mammoth desk. It always made me feel like I was five years old again withstanding his scrutiny. The man never spoke with me about anything but business. Definitely no Father of the Year Awards coming his way. Did he even love me? I knew he loved my mother, but me? I was not certain. He never said it, and I stopped asking why. It hurt less that way.

"You knew?" I questioned him. I realized word traveled fast and furious in our underground haven, but this had to be a record. Although, the general's daughter sentenced to be a Breeder had probably been the most exciting news in a decade, especially here lately. It was a far cry from our daily death-toll reports. News at eleven, who gets to bed the general's ice-maiden daughter.

"Of course I did. Did you think the Council would

not inform me of their decision concerning one of my platoon leaders?" He stared, impatience stamped across his stern features. His gray mustache twitched.

Or your daughter, I left that unsaid.

What would it take for him to give a shit? Would he be proud once I had birthed the next generation? Because everything I had done thus far, clawing my way up through the ranks, making myself the best damn soldier, appeared to be for naught. Even after all this time, his caustic remarks made my soul bleed.

"So you are fine with the fact that the Council gave Cade an all-access pass to rape me whenever he sees fit?"

I studied his reaction. He didn't even flinch.

"We all must do our duty. This is yours and that of any remaining female of an age able to bear children."

Cold bastard.

"But what about my platoon? I'm the best you've got, and you fucking know it. You need my platoon on this scouting mission to stop Drystan's bastards in their tracks, not getting bedded by Cade," I yelled. I'd never let my anger with him show, but the pent-up frustration seethed and engulfed me.

"Say the word, General," I said, "and I can have my men suited up within the hour. We can provide the bomb squad with the precise locations of the jump points and help protect them as they set the explosives. That is where I am needed." I craved action, with the desire to pummel something into dust. There was more to life than this. There had to be. I did not want to be dead inside like so many of the women I knew. Drones who bowed and scraped for their protector's affection. I did not need or want their so-called protection. I could bloody well protect myself better than any man. What I needed was my freedom, my ability to choose my fate instead of it being laid at my feet.

"My best? That remains to be seen. If that's the case, then you would follow my orders and that of the Council without question. Then we wouldn't be having this discussion, and you would be in your room with Cade doing your duty. I have already sent part of your squad out with Rick Sloan, from Cade's unit, as temporary commander of the Green Squad, until I make the decision to promote one of your majors. Part of Cade's squad is escorting the Council on the morrow to Versailles, and you better be well on your way to being pregnant by then." He coldly assessed me, no hint of warmth in his gaze. Maybe it would have been better if Drystan's armies had wiped the globe clean of the human race, if this was what we had become. I could not fathom my father betraying me like this, after all we had been through together. He reassigned my squad—to Rick Sloan, one of Cade's men, no less—without the courtesy of informing me first. I had not even been provided the civility of telling my men myself.

"How could you remove me from my squad? And then let them mate me with Cade?" I asked, choking on my words. Tears pricked the corners of my eyes. It was unfathomable. I blinked back the tears, unwilling to falter under his intense scrutiny. Weakness of any variety was unacceptable in a platoon commander, although I guess that did not apply to me any longer. I was a leader of no one.

"Because I suggested he would be the one best suited," he replied simply. Case closed, no further arguments necessary on my part.

Sweet merciful goddess!

I was surprised I was still standing. In a single swipe, he had metaphorically punched a hole clean through my chest. He had suggested Cade to the Council? I knew the Coven Mother had become my father's mate with the death of the previous high commander and held sway now with the way she voted, but to cast my fate into Cade's hands . . . I reeled at the thought. My simple world, the one I understood, had been upended and I grasped at the falling pieces.

"How could you sell me out? And to him? How could you?" I cursed myself for the trembling emotions. The vacuum of my world shrank into darkness, and my head swam with the implications. I had always believed, for all his gruffness, that my father had my back, that it was one of the reasons I had remained unmatched for so long. Could it be he had just placed me on reserve until another more-able-bodied male candidate appeared to step into my position? How could I have been so stupid and smug in my belief?

"Wake up, girl. Humanity is on the brink of extinction. We need every able-bodied female reproducing and replenishing our ranks. Even now, Amelia has the Coven working on an aging potion to help speed the growth process for children. The Densare needs more fighters if we are to survive this war, and you want to bandy wits about why? Wake the fuck up."

"Screw that! If Mom were alive, you wouldn't do this. And our numbers have made a comeback." I did not care for his reasons. What about my choice? I could not get past the fact he'd sold me out to Cade. He cared nothing for me, other than what I could do to breed more Cantati.

Fuck that.

"First, you missed the report from General Rémy. If you had appeared in my office five minutes earlier, you would have heard that they lost more than seventeen hundred at the Versailles Compound this week alone. Second"—he stepped around his desk and approached me until we stood toe-to-toe—"if your mother were alive, she'd tie you to the bed to ensure you did your duty to your people. Report to your room, I'll see that Cade meets you there once his mission has been completed, and do not emerge until you are with child. That's an order, Alana." For the first time in forever, he addressed me by name, instead of by rank. His stern features did not waiver and any hope I had held that there was some way out of my predicament sputtered and died.

"Yes, sir," I bit out as I saluted and quit his office. The threat of tears scorched the backs of my eyelids. Cold steel chains wrapped themselves about my wrists and shackled me to my fate.

Goddess help me.

CHAPTER THREE

I BLASTED THROUGH the Command Center as I left my father's office and almost barreled into Declan, a giant of a man barely a sliver older than I. Yet my anger seethed and coiled like a living, breathing being. Declan averted his eyes, slipping to the right to avoid my wrath.

"Sorry, sir." He saluted.

"Private." I returned his salute and continued marching past the radar screens and blinking lights. Would I be barred from returning to this room? Everything I held most dear had been whisked from my grasp. My breathing was shallow as I attempted to contain my fury. I should be out there fighting, protecting the remaining survivors, especially when Versailles had lost seventeen hundred people last week.

When I emerged through the Center doors, I hesitated. The hallway to the right led to the barracks and my room. The same room Cade would visit upon completing his assignment. Going left would take me to the cafeteria, the then training rooms, armory, and training fields.

I went left. Orders be damned. Consequences be damned. The Desert seemed preferable than my current predicament.

I strode through the crowded mess hall. The voices of the men there were a dull roar. I avoided eye contact. I did not want to witness their pity, or curiosity, or worse, their satisfaction. Conversation stopped as I passed. I wondered how fast my disobedience would be reported. I would kick their asses for the offense.

Like I give a shit what they think of me.

I was finished with them all. Maybe I would leave and head into the desert, or better yet stage a mutiny and start my own damn compound. I kept my features frozen and unreadable while striding through the maze. My fate was already the gossip of the Compound, why provide them with more fodder? But I should have gone the long way around to the training center. When I got angry, my rational brain tended to shut down and I was all rage, tossing any common sense into the trash.

Leaving the cafeteria, I marched into the hallway beyond and did not glance back as conversation resumed.

Vultures.

I breathed a sigh of relief as I entered the empty training room. Most Cantati were either on duty or in the mess hall at this hour. The Levare and other humans were not allowed in the Cantati training areas. The Mutari had created more than the Cantati. It had created another subset of humans. Similar to the Cantati, something within the human genetic coding had mutated and produced the race of the Levare, whose intelligence was only marginally higher than cows'. The Levare served the Cantati and did the most menial of jobs: cooking, cleaning, minding the fields and animals. And the rest, the humans who did not become Cantati or Levare, were given the jobs the Levare's lower intelligence could not handle. They trained in rebuilding our computer infrastructure, became doctors, builders constructing better walls to restrain demons, enforcers reporting to the Council and the Coven.

The gym had a large selection of free weights, weight machines, and punching bags dangling from support beams along the far wall. In the next room, the Cantati had practice dummies for sparring. I was at home here. This place made sense. The world outside these two rooms housed nothing but chaos. I smiled and headed for one of the bags. Stripping my jacket off, I wrapped tape around my hands with methodical precision. Once they were firmly bound, I allowed all the pent-up fury to explode and took my frustration out on the bag.

Uppercut, double jab, right hook, my hands burned with every throw. Overhand right, cross-punch right, left jab, right jab, check hook. I lost myself in the movements. My mind emptied with every hit, every kick.

A hand clasped my shoulder, and I swiveled, landing a right hook square onto Ben's jaw. His six-foot frame stumbled back and he held his clean-shaven jaw.

"Christ, Lieutenant!" Ben barked. His blue eyes, normally full of mischief, appeared dazed.

"Fuck, Ben! Don't sneak up on me like that." He knew better than that. I had a nasty right hook that would have knocked a lesser man unconscious.

"I didn't sneak. I had been calling your name for two minutes." He shook his head like he was attempting to shake off the effects of the punch. A red patch bloomed on his jaw. He would have a nasty bruise by tomorrow.

Mortified, I apologized. "Sorry about that."

"I'll live. The bag, however, is dead." Ben chuckled. I glanced over my shoulder. The bag looked like a grenade had ripped it to shreds.

"Your point?" I addressed him drolly. I had had a sucktacular day and did not need to explain my actions. As close as I was to these guys, even as their former leader, I could never falter in their eyes. No matter what I felt, no matter how torn up I was inside, I had been their direct superior, leader of the Green Squad. Ben Callihan, Nick Frasella, Luke Holland, and Quinten Black had been my major squadron leaders. We fought together, bled together, and now at my lowest point, they came to offer support.

"We get it," Quinten chimed in. He was the most level-headed of the group. I wished the Council had considered him. Between his easy going nature, field expertise, and his smoldering good looks, I would have been hard-pressed to allow their decision rile me this much. At only five-eleven, he was a bit shorter than your average soldier, but he was solid, lean muscle. His darker features spoke of some Spanish or Italian ancestry, not that anyone really knew anymore. He kept his dark hair cut short, but the hint of curls remained.

"And we don't like that you've been handed off to that bastard any more than you do," Luke insisted. My other candidate was a blond-haired, blue-eyed, six-two stud muffin. He wore fatigues better than any man in the company, as far as I was concerned. He had a bit more bulk than Quinten, shoulders a bit wider, and frankly made my mouth water when I allowed myself to think of him in any way other than one of my officers.

"Yeah, but you don't have to sleep with him." The four men looked like they had swallowed robin's eggs at my retort. Shame washed over me. "Never mind."

It wasn't their fault, but mine. I focused on the job and rarely lifted my head up for air. So it was no wonder that the ability to make decisions for my life had been removed and I felt all the control slipping through my grasp faster than it took SPD to distort a memory.

I had made the mistake of hesitating and should have chosen one of these fine men before the Council had issued its verdict. Luke or Quinten would have been the better choices, but Ben and Nick would have done in a pinch. None of that mattered now.

"Why aren't you out on patrol?" I asked, unwrapping the tape from my hands.

"Rick Sloan took half of the squad and had the rest of us stay to defend the Compound." Quinten replied.

"So did you come to console me or is there something you guys need?" I prayed to the gods for something else to deal with other than this pressure in my chest that felt like a balloon was about to pop.

"We think platoons of demons are on the move. And we wanted to hunt them down before they do any damage," Ben remarked.

"Where'd you get your intel?" I almost salivated over the news. That's what I needed to rid myself of this tension. I was such a hypocrite. I adored terminating demons as much as Cade did, perhaps even more, only I didn't collect trophies. Maybe that's why he scared the bloody hell out of me. With Cade, the darkness that had always been present within me, snaking its way through my soul, would be given free rein. It would consume me in large unyielding and unending gulps. It was a place from which there was no coming back. I would plunge headlong into the murky waters and be forever altered. I feared that more than I feared death, more than I feared losing my freedom. I could never let the darkness win.

They all pointed at Luke, our demon-detecting surveillance god.

Luke and I had a similar specialty. I could find demons' energy signatures like a tracer, but I had no idea the numbers or exactly where, unless I was within five miles of them. He could locate them on a map of the world and provide precise locations, numbers and, on some rare occasions, the breed. The big difference was that his power was useless without a map, so out in the field, his talents were a bust. Which was where I tended to come in, built-in demon detector and all. My powers were comparable to a metal detector. My senses picked up those evil bastards' energy, and allowed my squad to home in and destroy them.

"Intel came into the Command Center that demons have regrouped and are advancing on the wall. General O'Hare asked me to check with my powers. They are gathering in larger numbers than I have ever sensed before. And they are not far outside the wall."

"Did the general send out a squad to The Wall to check it out?" I had never known Luke to be off by much. If what he had detected was true, then we had scores of demons headed our way. Granted, Cade's squad was battle ready, and my men were nothing to sneeze at either, but if it were true, we needed everyone for this fight.

"He didn't think the intel was correct and didn't

want to risk lives. Cade's squad was sent into the Desert to find the jump point."

Bleeding Christ! That left only half of my squad protecting The Wall! And with an officer I wouldn't trust with a potato gun.

This was not information the general could ignore. What was he thinking? Had Amelia persuaded him to play it safe? If Luke knew where they were located, I would defy the Council and scout the area. They needed my skills. They could prove to be the thing that kept our people from complete annihilation.

"You've got the location?" *Please let him have it.* I could save my people and use it to extinguish my fury at the same time. The focus of a search-and-destroy mission where I could unload my fury, my grief, onto the enemy would go a long way toward calming the turbulent mine field of my emotions.

"Yep, southwest of the wall." Luke smiled smugly. He knew me too well, knew how much I thrived on this action. And had handed me a way to salvage my dignity amidst the fraying ends of my sanity.

"Let's go get them," I ordered, exhilarated by the prospect. When it came to war, the importance of even one extra soldier could mean the difference between this Compound surviving or perishing. I was fully prepared to disobey orders to ensure my people lived.

"We'll go, but you shouldn't buck the Council's orders." Nick, the youngest of the group, and a ginger, cautioned restraint. The problem was, I did not have any. I needed this mission more than I needed to follow the rules. If we were caught, I would deal with the consequences. They were all agog for my womb and wanted it too damn badly.

Luke and I had a wordless conversation. He understood the ramifications of this mission and was on board. I glanced at Ben and Quinten. They both nodded their acquiescence. They would march into hell beside me if it came down to it. Nick had earned his spot through his skills, but was still uncomfortable bucking the system.

"Major Frasella, I'm going, period. If there are as many demons advancing on the wall as Luke detected, then we will need every soldier regardless of the Council's orders. We leave within the hour. I'll slip out unseen after I get my gear and meet you at the first rendezvous point just past the Compound at Lower Thames Street. The guards tend to be a little more lax at the gate, and that will provide the best route for us to take. That route should keep us from running into Cade's squad and the rest of ours under Rick's leadership. Our mission is to assess the situation and bring back concrete intelligence to the general." If we were caught, I would ensure my squad was not punished.

"Thought you might say that." Quinten tossed a black gym bag at my feet. The top was open and I spied all my gear plus weapons. I could have kissed him for this.

A smile spread across my lips as excitement pumped through my veins. I lived for this.

"Suit up, boys."

"Hoorah," they shouted in unison.

CHAPTER FOUR

WE EMERGED FROM the Tower like ghostly apparitions, the five of us keeping to the building's shadows in a staggered wedge formation. The setting sun glinted off the high window panes of the former office buildings we passed. Our tiny scouting party remained silent and surveyed for any returning battalions, mainly Cade's bunch, as we headed in the direction of our objective. We were going to scout Hyde Park for the enemy subversives Luke had picked up and eliminate any attempting a wall breach.

Lower Thames Street followed the Thames River, leaving our hunting party without cover to the south. Using the buildings that were still standing for cover, I conveyed all orders wordlessly. My men were trained well, and we functioned like clockwork with Quinten taking up point while the rest of us followed his lead.

"Lieutenant." Nick's voice broke the silence.

"What, Frasella?" I winced and scoped out the intersection we were about to cross. I did not want anyone coming across our recon squad. We were far enough from the Command Center that our voices would not carry, I hoped. In this place, sound carried.

"Who do you think they will make lieutenant since you are … you know?" Red crept into his face, and he shuffled his feet.

"About to breed the next generation?" I could barely keep the sarcasm from my voice.

"Yeah." Even in the darkening twilight, I noticed the red in his cheeks. Nick was in many ways still too young for the mantle that had been placed upon his shoulders. We all were. With the enlistment age lowered to sixteen to swell our ranks, at twenty he was old by comparison. Although by his age I had already made lieutenant.

"I'm not sure. General O'Hare made Rick Sloan acting lieutenant until a decision is made. Though I don't know that it will matter if the Council has someone else in mind." And didn't that just burn my gullet. Like the general thought highly of my input. Today had been an exercise in how little my opinion mattered.

"Oh." He shifted his attention back to our trek as our company turned off Lower Thames Street onto Northumberland and plunged into a maze of buildings. We maneuvered, as we had hundreds of times, into ranger file as we passed corners stained with blood, buildings charred and bullet-ridden from prior battles. Most of the buildings we crept past were mere hollow shells, used for nothing more than defensive cover from our enemy. Otherwise, the general would have had them demolished years ago.

Who would the general promote in my stead? Certainly not Nick. He was far too green and did not comprehend what a position like this exacted from the bearer. I glanced at Ben as he secured the crossroads and waved us on through, sardonic grin across his face. Ben was too reckless. He would plunge into a nest of Efrits without having a clear strategy for escape.

That left Luke and Quinten. Both men were exceptional soldiers. Luke was the hero, though, the all-star golden boy who could do no wrong. The men he led were like devotees to a god and worshiped the ground he walked on. He was a sound candidate for replacing me. My only concern was that he took risks so he could play the hero. I did not believe it was a conscious action, more ingrained in his being. The problem was, when men's lives were in your hands, the wrong decision could get them killed. And sometimes, it meant your decisions were second-guessed by others, but in my book if you could sleep at night over the choices you made, you did the right thing.

Quinten would be the best choice by far. He wasn't a golden boy by a long shot. A very scrappy fighter, he had an intelligent mind that grasped situations often far beyond my understanding. He was calmer than the rest of them. I often considered him the scholar of the bunch. If our lives, and our world, had been different, I could picture him teaching a group of students in a university. When we were not training or on a mission such as this, he tended to be in a corner of the Tower grounds with a book he'd borrowed from the Council Library.

The five-mile route we chose would lead us far enough away from Cade's squad. I knew the paths to the wall by memory. My life, all of our lives, existed within ten miles: the wall was no more than a five-mile radius from the Compound. The majority of the buildings we passed were vacant. People were not willing to live outside the confines of the Compound any longer. When I was a child, these buildings had held life, where presently they were nothing more than tombs. They stood as blatant reminders of all humanity had lost.

Quinten, on point, signaled a halt at the last mile before we reached our objective rally point. Sending my feelers out for energy signatures, I came across only ours. As we neared the rally point, Quinten stayed on lead, while Ben, Luke, and Nick fanned out in a two, six, and ten o'clock formation. I brought up the rear of our company.

Quinten motioned forward with a flick of his wrist, and our company crept along the final alley that led to the wall. At the corner, Quinten came up short and held up his fist. I signaled for him to move forward, and he shook his head no.

And that's when I heard the clicking scrap of claws against pavement.

Bloody hell!

I needed to quit thinking about my impending motherhood and focus on the task before me. Otherwise, I would get my men killed. I dropped my shields, feeling for energy signatures. My internal siren blared code red at the sheer numbers in the alley. There had to be at least a dozen. I signaled the numbers to Luke and Ben with instructions to head back around and cut off the escape route for these things.

They nodded their understanding and took off down the direction we had come. This left me with Quinten and Nick. I caught Quinten's gaze, the warmth I usually saw replaced with a steely resolve. He'd do well as lieutenant if the general passed him the mantle.

A silent conversation passed between us.

Nick and I will ambush them on this side. You watch our six.

Agreed.

I nodded my head at his assent. I trusted his judgment at defending our backs more than Nick. It was not that Nick was competent, he was, but he was young enough, and cocky enough to make fatal mistakes.

I signaled Nick, and he fell into step beside me as we rounded the corner and came face-to-face with a dozen Hathas, Drystan's beefy foot soldiers, who stood over eight feet tall with arms the size of small trees. In the darkening twilight, their gray skin appeared spectral and made their black, razor-sharp tusks curling up from their bottom lips more menacing. With the way their tusks were formed, they always seemed to be growling, displaying rows of long, jagged teeth. When they saw us, they screeched and rushed toward us. The close confines of the alley made firing weapons unreliable at best. I unsheathed my long blade and attacked the brute nearest me.

I swiped at its midsection before it could place its hands on me. A trail of intestines followed in the wake of my blade. I heard Nick off to my right engaged with one of the beasts as I moved on to the next. New screeches emitted from the other end of the alley, and I smiled. Luke and Ben were silencing Hathas, too. These bastards would never get close enough to crush us.

The four of us dispatched all twelve Hathas while Quinten watched our backs for more that could be approaching. Ben and Luke met Nick and I in the middle of the pile of corpses. My sensors went haywire.

"Lieutenant," Quinten shouted, pointing to the tops of the buildings sandwiching the alley.

My heart stopped.

Demons snarled from the rooftops, surrounding our scouting party. There had to be fifty of them at least, a mix of breeds. I spied Yathuri with their blood-red eyes trained on us, their claws jutting from their hands, Efrits with their elongated snouts openly hissing, displaying rows of gleaming fangs, and more

Hathas. I heard the flapping of leathery wings and glanced skyward. The rising dark was obscured by the blackened bodies of Ahures.

Five against more than fifty. Even for a full squad, those would be crappy odds. I had to get my men out of there.

"Move," I ordered.

The nightmare poured over the rooftops and onto level ground, surrounding our hunting party. We formed a circle with our backs to each other. There were too many to take down with hand-to-hand combat. I nodded at Quinten and the rest of my men switched to their assault rifles. We had to risk the close confines. My men opened fire.

I yanked my .45 out and began firing rounds. All thoughts of Cade, the Coven, and the rest of my wretched life emptied with every kicking reverberation of my side-arm.

The Ahures dive-bombed our little party with talons extended. They liked to play with their prey and would snatch their victim up, fly them a hundred feet or so in the air, before dropping them to their death. Sick fuckers liked their meals as liquid pulp. I dropped my shoulders as one missed me by a few inches.

"Shit!" Nick screamed, and I heard him go down. Was he dead? I glanced back and saw him holding his shoulder. Not dead, but the Ahure's talons hurt like hell. The rest of us surrounded him as the demons caught scent of fresh human blood. Their actions became frenzied. I sensed their ever-present hunger. They thirsted for human blood the way we craved water.

Demon carcasses piled up around us, making movement difficult. If we stayed put, we would become this horde's next meal.

"We need to leave the alley," I bit out, striking my blade against a Yathuri's throat when a bullet failed to stop its advance.

"Christ, Lieutenant, there's nowhere to go, and we're surrounded. How the hell do you want us to accomplish that?" Ben huffed out, protesting as he wrestled with a Hatha.

"If we can remove ourselves from the confines of the alley, we can toss a few grenades to clear out the rest," I ordered, taking a page out of my father's book. "Quinten, Luke, I need you to push our advantage forward to the street. Ben, grab Nick. I'll bring up the rear. We need to move, now." I commanded.

"Let's do this," golden boy Luke affirmed.

As a unit, we fought. Their green serpentine blood caked our features as we forced a demon retreat. A bullet caught an Ahure between the eyes, and its head exploded. Only fifteen feet until we reached the street.

We jostled forward, claws swiped and clutched toward me.

"Duck!" Quinten boomed.

Heat blasted me as a fireball careened past my head and exploded up against the building's side. The flames snagged a few Hatha in the mix. Their dying screeches pierced my ears. It seemed a Feronte had joined the fray.

Oh, joy!

Our party pressed forward, firing at every demon in sight, until we emerged on the open street.

"Watch for friendlies." I heard an all too familiar voice behind our company. We were no longer on our own.

By the gods this was bad!

"What the devil are you doing out here?" I swiveled my head from the melee long enough to spy Cade, with his platoon of soldiers flanking his sides. Some of his men had already engaged with the enemy and leaped into combat.

"Get your balls out of their vise grip and help us out," I snapped. Man could take his rage and suck it up like a good little soldier.

Fury emanated from his solid frame as he engaged with a Yathuri. The look in his eyes told me in all of two seconds that there would be hell to pay for this jaunt. I had given him and the Council the proverbial finger. Would he cast me out and take me before the Council? A part of me hoped he would. Then I would at least be shod of him and good riddance.

I directed my gaze back to the two Ferontes who approached.

With no time left to consider the consequences, I jumped with my long blade, bringing the blade against the Feronte's neck, and watched its head tumble to the ground. The second Feronte died before it could unleash a screech in my direction.

With the added help from Cade's men, the remaining demons were exterminated with ease. Hands grappled me and yanked me from behind. Cade hauled me from the victory we had achieved here.

"You bitch." He snarled, shoving me toward the building. Any opportunities for a civilized conversation evaporated the moment he put his hands on me.

Sheathing my blade, I fought like a cat about to be dunked in a bucket full of water, focusing all my wrath, all my indignity on him. How could he think he could bully me like this, and in front of our squads? It didn't matter that I had been relieved of command, my men still respected me. I had been needed in this fight. I sucker-punched him with a right uppercut, and he responded in kind. It was no wonder I would never willingly submit my body to him. His left fist clipped my jaw, not really intending to hurt me, just stun me. It pissed me off more. I was not known for being levelheaded, but his blatant mockery of my skills and feinting an actual rebuttal to my assault was like tossing a lit match on a powder keg. Any common sense in my body fled, and I went for his jugular. I pounded on his chest and beat him back.

If he was surprised by the brutality of my assault, his gaze never faltered. His only aim was to secure the prize he'd won by order of the Council. I wanted a knock-down, drag-out fight, until the last one was still standing, and he gave me the neutered version.

Sadistic fucker.

I lunged forward with a kick that had brought down hulking demon brutes. Confidence bloomed that this parry would bring the smug bastard to his knees.

It did.

Except, then Cade withdrew from his pocket a small black device, no more than three inches long, and jabbed it against my exposed flesh through a tear in my pants. Volts of electricity sizzled and flashed throughout my body. It felt like thousands of nails being jammed into every inch of my body. I could focus on nothing but the searing, mind-numbing agony. The demon carcasses diminished, and I viewed the scene before me in a haze. Jaw clenched, I struggled against the anguish. My hands balled into fists as I collapsed on the ground.

Son of a bitch had Tasered me.

While my body trembled from the remaining electricity sizzling in my system, he hoisted me up, tossing me over his shoulder. His lengthy strides removed me from my men. And I could do nothing but clasp him more firmly as he spirited me away.

CHAPTER FIVE

PRISON CELLS AT the Compound were not much different than regular rooms. The only structural differences were the bars across the door and the dirt floor, but other than that, they were rather cozy. The dank walls held the stench of the Thames below, never quite losing that musty, stale scent.

It had been twelve hours since Cade and my father had locked me in here. Twelve hours since I had last spied my squad leaders as they were led away in handcuffs. Twelve hours for the Council to decide my fate, yet again.

Being trapped was worse in my mind than a sentence to the Desert. At least in the Desert, a body withstood a chance, slim as it might be, for survival. In here, locked in, all a person could do was await their fate, instead of fighting to change it.

I licked my parched lips for what must be the hundredth time. They had long since cracked, and in the corner I tasted dried blood. I had bit the inside of my lip during the worst of the electrically induced tremors.

I had had no visitors, no food, no water, no bloody warmth in this hovel since Cade had dumped my body here. One would think that they would at least give a prisoner a blanket or a fire. Although, I think they did that on purpose. This way, when a person went before the Council, they were willing to agree to anything as long as they did not have to journey back to their cell.

Footsteps stomped against stone, and I knew my time in this place was finished. Where would the Council send me? To Cade or the Desert?

My prison bars swung inward, and Cade's men surrounded me. No Cade. So the sadistic bastard didn't have the balls to face me himself. He sent ten armed men to escort me to the Council, I presumed, but couldn't be bothered with me himself. It made me feel all warm and fuzzy that he thought it would take that many men to keep little me in line. As for Cade, that man would rue today's transgressions, make no mistake. I would never allow him anywhere near my body, at least not willingly. The Council might disagree on that matter.

Walking to a Council hearing with armed guards was never a good sign. If this was how it would be? Then my actions, regardless that they were made for the greater good of the Compound, had made me an enemy of the Council.

Figures. Bloody hell, if I survived this one intact it would be a wonder.

"Move." Rick Sloan nudged me forward at gun point. If my fate didn't dangle precariously over the edge of no return, I would show this idiot how we did things in my squad. He jabbed me again. Either I moved or the man would put a crater in my back and end my apparent futile rebellion. How the hell had my life barreled so far out of hand? I was not attempting to start a revolution. I just wanted to live on my terms, not the Council's.

A third, firmer nudge against my already bruised ribs and I picked up my feet.

Better to get the bloody inquisition over with than stoke the Council's ire even more than I had already. Would they make an example out of me, punish me more fiercely than most to serve as a warning to the rest of what happened when a person resisted their system? I blinked as the light in the hallway battered my gaze. We marched onward through the familiar twists and turns of the underground Compound, past the half-expectant faces of residents who waited with bated breath to see what the general's disobedient offspring would conspire to do next. I took none of it in. I let their rapt gazes fall upon me like leaves in a stern wind.

The soldiers led me to the Council chambers. The guards standing watch opened the double steel doors at my approach.

"Alana Devereaux, Your Grace." One of the guards announced me at the threshold of the chamber.

"Come forward," Amelia demanded the silk of her voice encased in steel.

Head held high, I ambled into the chamber. The door closed with a resounding thud behind me.

"Ah yes, Miss Devereaux, we meet again so soon. Perhaps the last time you were here you misunderstood the Council's directive."

"No, ma'am."

"Ah, so then you intentionally defied the Council and committed more than four acts of treason against your brethren."

I sucked in a swift breath. Treason. When had defying orders become treason? Would they imprison me for life, using me solely for breeding purposes, or exile me? I wondered why I had spent so much time in a cell when it seemed my fate and my acts had already been judged. This meeting appeared to be more of a formality, a way to assuage the masses the Council presided over to convince them that the stringent dictatorship of laws was just.

"No, not intentionally." I wanted to scream at them, rail against them for the unfairness of it all.

"So you admit you defied the Council." *By the goddess.* The Coven Mother clearly wanted to convict me. Why? Because I'd defied their edict?

"Yes." I hissed and felt the nails being driven into

my coffin. I should just go dig my grave in the common yard. It was to be exile for sure. Never mind the hundreds of lives I likely helped save, nor the countless missions I had engaged in that had protected the very laws they held so dear.

"And your majors. Did they commit treason with you?" I felt faint as she threw down a gauntlet I had not expected. Why penalize my men? They had only been following my orders. Granted, I had been removed from command, but that was a tiny technicality. The Council could punish me all they wanted, but my men were off-limits. They evidently did not understand the brevity of the mission we undertook. They lived because of us.

I glanced around the room at the stone faces before me. Yes, I had willfully denied the Council and butted against their system, but never at the cost of my men's freedom or their lives.

I swallowed my pride and pleaded with the Council. "No. Please don't punish them. They were following my orders. Do with me what you will, but leave them out of this."

"Your men will be dealt with," Amelia stated, as if their sentences had already been decided.

I paled. How could I be so stupid that I put my men at risk?

"I'm sorry. Please, they had nothing to do with this. Send me into exile or imprison me, but reassign them, put them on latrine duty. No one should be banished but me."

Amelia held up her fine-boned hand, magic pulsing from her palm.

"Silence."

I could not speak if I tried. The Coven Mother had spelled me with a flick of her wrist.

"The Council has agreed that you are henceforth banned from Cantati Forces. You shall be transported from Council chambers to your room, where Cade McDonnell awaits your presence. That is where you will remain until you're with child. If, for any reason, you must leave your room, you shall be accompanied by armed guards. Is that understood?"

In all the commotion, I had forgotten one thing: my womb was far too valuable for them to toss me into the Desert. Power. I had it and had failed to use it. Amelia flicked her wrist and removed the charm.

"Yes," I blurted out but stayed further words. My guys' lives were far too precious to me to cause them further harm. The Council had me, and by the gleam in the Coven Mother's eyes, she knew it. Even if she were bluffing, she knew I would never intentionally risk their lives.

"You are dismissed. Guards, take her to her room."

Four soldiers, supplied to the hilt with weaponry, surrounded me. They were ready to lead me to Cade.

"Oh and Alana," Amelia purred with an edge of ice belying the sugary coating.

"Yes?" I shivered. She had trumped me in every way possible. What further recourse could she have?

"Any further infractions, and the Council will expel your entire squad into the Desert in your stead."

CHAPTER SIX

That bitch!

SHE UTILIZED MY softness for my squad to control me, to force me to submit to their decree that I allow Cade to impregnate me. I hoped the Coven Mother burned in hell for this one and let her know it with my glare.

"Good, I see we understand each other," Amelia replied.

"We do." I turned away from her, rattled by the strength of the woman's hatred for me and fueled by the urge to retaliate. If not for the threat she posed to my men, I would have given in to the urge to punch her until I felt better.

I marched toward the door, and the guards raced to catch up.

"After you." I let the first two pass as we walked into the hallway. It was not every day that a prisoner galloped to their punishment. Which was why the men at my sides continued glancing my way, as if they expected me to sprout horns and a tail. It was mere self-preservation, for not only myself but my men. Amelia had upped the ante and called my bluff better than any cardsharp. She knew I would not risk the lives of the men who served under me.

The trek to my room was way too brief. Before I could turn the knob on my door, one of my keepers did the deed for me.

Cade stood amidst my meager belongings, dominating them. The rage I had witnessed near the wall was barely contained behind a sheen of civility. No one discerned the menace but me. There would be no aid this night.

"Come in." He held the door open farther for me. For the rest of the group, he appeared the concerned mate, ready to forgive my crimes. When that could not be further from the truth. The unknown nature of his retribution sent slithers of apprehension through my system. I could handle myself in any situation, any circumstances that I could fight my way through. Except I could not fight him, could not defend myself in any way against him. Otherwise my men paid the price. What's more, by the glean in his eyes, he knew he had won.

"That will be all this evening. Please don't disturb us for any reason, regardless of what you hear." He winked at his men, who masked their chortles with coughs.

My cheeks flamed as I passed across the

threshold. He had blatantly told these men exactly what he planned to do with me tonight. I was not virginal by any stretch of the mind, but I had never been free with my body. He had all but smacked my ass and staked his claim in front of them.

Bastard.

I would never be his. My body, yes, but my soul …

Never.

I stopped short at the sight of my bed, the navy covers turned down in anticipation. The door slammed shut with a resounding thud. Metal screeched as he secured a deadbolt and trapped me inside. I did not move, just waited for him to pounce. My breath caught in my throat, and I squeezed my eyes shut.

Fingers dug into my jaw and tilted my head back.

"Look at me."

I ignored him, keeping my eyes closed.

The rage I had only sensed in him exploded, and I found myself pressed up against the wall with one hand around my throat while the other was clenched like talons around my face.

"Look at me," He growled, and his hot breath washed over me.

I cracked my eyes open and poured every ounce of my hatred into that one glance.

"You will never pull a stunt like you did yesterday. Do you understand? I wanted to be nice, give you a chance to get used to the idea of our situation, but you have forced my hand. You are to shower and rid your form of dungeon stench. You will return to this room without a single stitch of clothing on and lie on the bed. Tonight and every night from here on out, you will fuck me as if your life depends upon it. From here on out, you will not wear clothes unless I desire it. You will not eat or sleep unless I make it so. And I can promise you this, Alana, if you ever pull a stunt like that again, I will give you the spanking you so richly deserve and then fuck you anyway."

He released my body, although I remained up against the wall. Would he really give me a few minutes?

"Go," he ordered and pointed to the bathroom. "Leave the door open."

With every ounce of bravado left within my arsenal, I side stepped him and marched to my bathroom. Although, not before I noticed the rather large bulge in his pants. I wanted to vomit.

This was truly happening. Cade would, as he said, fuck me. I did not realize I was shaking until I attempted to unzip my pants. My hands shook so violently the zipper became stuck midway down. Knowing the small bit of time he afforded me was limited, I squeezed myself out of my pants with the zipper only halfway undone.

The shower was lukewarm, but it was more than I had experienced in days. There was something so primal about what a shower did for a body. Slicking off the dirt and grime from the last few days, I decided my hair needed a good washing as well. My teeth chattered from the tepid water but I did not care. Closing my eyes I stood underneath the spray and let the water rinse the last suds from my body.

Resolved at the night to come, I opened my eyes to shut the water off. Cade stood half-dressed on the other side of the shower glass, watching me. There was not an inch of fat on his body. It was all sculpted muscle with whorls of dark hair dusting his chest. His eyes burned in blatant male hunger. His eyes feasted on my naked form and the bulge in his low-slung pants strained against the material.

I should be worshiping his body and thanking my lucky stars to have a man in such fine physical form as to be descended from the gods. I should want him. Any other woman would rejoice and anticipate the night ahead. But not me.

He adjusted his hard flesh.

Repulsed, I twisted the knob, cutting off the water flow. Cade had the shower door open before I could blink. Uncaring of my wet form, he yanked me from the shower. My damp flesh met his heated, rock-hard form and shivered. His eyes smoldered, thinking I anticipated his attentions. It could not have been further from the truth. Hatred boiled in my gullet. If it hadn't been for the death threat hanging over my men's heads, I would have ended Cade here and now.

I started to pull away. To do what, I had no idea. All I knew was that I detested his hands on me, wanted to gouge his eyes out and keep them from my naked body.

His powerful hands stalled my backward progression and propelled my body up alongside his. "Remember," he chewed out, "your life and those of your squad leaders depend upon your performance."

Hatred burned inside. I would kill him for this violation. I had to perform otherwise my men would be exiled. I sliced off my turbulent emotions at the knees. I lifted my hands to his chest.

"Yes, I remember," I responded, my voice sounding detached, covering the boiling disgust I felt, like I was a robotic doll.

Cade smiled in apparent victory. He carried me into his bedroom and laid me upon the bed. His mouth descended, claiming my parted lips as his big body followed mine onto the bed. His hands were everywhere, stroking, petting. His fingers cupped my breasts, and he moaned, grinding his hips against me. He reached for the zipper of his pants.

Sirens blared. Furious pounding sounded on my door.

"Fuck! This better be important." Cade withdrew from my body and the bed.

"Cover yourself," he growled, marching to the door.

Spurred into action, I yanked the covers up around my form as he opened the door.

"What?" Cade snarled at Quinten and three of Cade's men.

All four had a direct line of sight of me in bed, and I felt my cheeks heat. It was bad enough for them to know in theory that I was Cade's bed partner, now they had an eagle's-eye view.

"Drystan's armies are moving against the city, sir. General O'Hare requested your presence in the Command Center," Quinten replied. He handed him a missive, which I assumed was from the general.

Cade crumpled the orders between his Herculean hands.

"Give me five minutes." And he slammed the door in their faces.

A lesser woman would have cowered against the wall. Everything in my being defied him and rejoiced in his thwarted attempt to claim me. The gods had granted me a reprieve, and I had to bite my lips to keep the smile from my face.

He glanced sharply at me and pointed a finger toward me.

"Don't think this is over. We will be picking up right where we left off. And I mean exactly where we left off, with my dick about to slide into your tight cunt." He snarled in apparent sexual frustration. I watched him calculate the general's ire should he not report immediately and deemed it unworthy of potentially losing his prize.

In under three minutes, he was fully clothed and

armed. While I remained with my covers up to my chin.

He stomped over and hauled me up. The blankets slipped from my grasp. He drew me close, and his lips claimed mine.

"Don't even think of rebutting me or leaving this room," he ordered gutturally as he withdrew from me on a moan.

He tossed me back on the bed and headed for the door, uncaring of the state of my undress. Bastard would likely parade me naked through the Compound if he could to show off his prize. I scrambled for the covers and yanked them over my breasts as his door swung open.

He glanced back and then at Quinten. "See that she does not leave this room for ANY reason, or I will ensure that you find yourself in the Desert. You three, with me."

He strode from the room without a backward glance not even bothering to shut the door for he knew I would not leave. Quinten's kind eyes were more than I could handle.

I shattered like glass in a window-pane.

CHAPTER SEVEN

"ARE YOU ALRIGHT?" Quinten asked above the din of air-raid sirens, the same ones the British had used during World War II when the Germans were bombing London. It always struck me as odd the methods that humans had developed to defend themselves from other humans.

He trod into my room, closing the door behind him. I lay crumpled on the bed awash in tears. Grief choked my response, and it sounded like a garbled mess even to my ears. After every horror I had survived, this was the worst. In every other instance, I had been resolute with the knowledge that I had the power to beat back any enemy.

What do you do when the enemy was not only allowed, but encouraged, to strip you of any last shred of yourself? I hated Cade. I wanted to wash his stench from my body, but I knew deep down it was a move in futility. He wanted to possess my body, and if I weren't careful, he would destroy my soul. Then I would truly become one of them, a Breeder, whose listless existence rose and set with her protector. I would kill him before I allowed him to turn me into that. I had no idea how or when, but make no mistake, I would see him dead. With any luck, he would not return from his mission. It happened all the time. I prayed to the gods that he would meet his fate.

I flinched at Quinten's hand at my shoulder and gazed into his concerned features.

"Alana, how can I help?" he murmured. I opened my mouth to reply, but no sound came out. Tears blurred my vision, and I felt him wrap the blankets securely around my form before he put his arms around me. He scooted us over and rested his back against the wall.

I never cried. The last time was when my mother died.

Quinten held me, just like that. He gave comfort as I emptied all my sorrows. He was my rock as the storm of my emotions battered me. Through all of it, he stroked my arm and stood as bastion against the dark swelling tide.

"Alana?" He had stilled his movements.

"Hmm?" I retreated slightly from his arms, a little surprised by how much I enjoyed the comfort within them.

"What if I went before the Council?" He hesitated, searching my face. What did he hope to find there? His stoic face, ever the scholar, studied my reaction.

"And told them what?" I could usually read people, but his intentions were shrouded and gave me pause.

"What if I told them you were mine before they issued their order mating you to Cade?" he asked, half expectant, hope swimming to the surface in his gaze.

"No. You know the Council would punish you, not to mention Cade would kill you for the offense. As much as I want to rid myself of him, it's not worth your life." I could never make him pay for my mistakes. No matter how much I wanted my freedom.

"If you weren't my superior officer, I would have made advances a long time ago. I love you. I have for some time. Now, as to Cade and the Council, let me handle them."

I gasped at his confession. Hope bubbled. He loved me. I had not heard those words since I was a child. While I may not love him, I did care for him. We were friends, had always worked seamlessly together in the field. Was there a chance I could feel more for him?

Yes.

His face was inches from mine, and in the space of a heartbeat, his lips claimed mine. For a half second, I did not move, too stunned by his declaration and the potency of his emotions as they swept over me. Then my shock bled into need, and I moaned. My hands caressed his face, stroking his cheeks, noticing the stubble along his jaw. He held my mouth prisoner against his as he delved deeper, his tongue tangling with mine.

Love. It did not exist in our world, and yet here was Quinten professing it. Why hadn't I chosen him? I had known that the Council would force my hand eventually, and if I had made a choice, all of this could have been avoided. I may not be in love with Quinten, but I did have feelings for him. Could I allow him to save me, when it could cost him his life?

I could feel his rising excitement at our exchange, even though he never touched more than my head. Putting a hand against his solid chest, I pushed back, ending the kiss. The hungry, possessive look on his face sealed my decision.

"I can't let you do this." Cade would kill him, period. He already felt he owned me and would fight like a rabid dog to keep his claim.

"Yes, you can. I want to. I should have done it a year ago."

"Quinten, as much as I want to rid myself of Cade, I couldn't let you risk your life when I don't feel the same. I care about you. You're my friend, but it would be selfish of me to ask this of you." I winced inside. I hated hurting him. And I could tell that my words had diminished some of the fervor from his features.

"It doesn't matter. I'm going before the Council anyway. I love you enough for the both of us. Give me a chance. Besides, wouldn't you rather sleep with your friend than a man you hate?"

I was not worthy of him. He meant it, though. Every word. His earnest emotions fueled the hope surging in my chest.

"Okay," I agreed.

Quinten looked as though I had just handed him a fortune and he wanted to build a shrine in my honor. I was not worthy of his worship. But I would strive every day to feel something for him, to try to love him. It was the least I could do, given what he was willing to face for me.

How could I do this to him? How could I ask him to face the Council and go up against Cade's might? I couldn't let him fight Cade. He was a vicious warrior. Terror seized me. We were both about to commit treason, but for real this time.

"But promise me ..."

"Anything," he swore, tracing his hands over my arms.

"Stay away from Cade. He's not worth potential recourse by the Council."

"After what he did to you tonight, absolutely fucking not. That bastard will get what he deserves."

Horrified, I said, "No, you can't go gunning for him. He wasn't able to consummate our union. You stopped him, saved me just in time. I won't do this, if that is your plan. I can't risk you."

"Fine."

"Just like that?" I asked, feeling uneasy. He had

agreed without much of a fight. I wasn't sure I trusted his response.

"Yep, just like that," he replied firmly, without hesitation. His thumb traced my lips as if he memorized their shape with his gentle caress.

"Why? When you know you will be facing …" I gulped and closed my eyes. *Please let me fall in love with this man!* He was too good for me. It shamed me that all I could muster for him was friendly fondness. Shoving any guilt aside, I vowed to make myself love him to repay him. Because I knew after tonight, I would never be able to submit myself to Cade's demands.

"Like I said before, I have wanted you for forever, it seems. Besides, I'm not getting a bad bargain out of it. I'll get you." He kissed me again with a smile in his eyes.

"I wish you would have made those advances." I smiled sadly before continuing. "The Council will not be gentle and will likely question the two of us fiercely. They will check my body for signs that I am no longer a maiden."

"Zarek, huh? He took it." He showed no hint of surprise. And here I thought we had succeeded in keeping our rendezvous a secret. My guys knew me well.

I nodded in the affirmative. He might as well know what he was getting with me, for all the trouble my actions would cause him.

"Did you tell anyone?"

"No, and then he …"

"Died." He seemed more pleased with the circumstances than I figured he would be.

"Yes. You do realize we will be lying under oath to the Council. If they rule against"

"I told you," he interrupted, "I have no problem with it. And I will make sure the others corroborate our story."

"But what will we tell the Council? They will question why we didn't come forward before they made their ruling." Amelia, especially, would see through any flimsy excuse. The others could be swayed, but that one? She had it out for me and was the only Council member who worried me.

"We tell them that we are madly in love and that you didn't want me to get in trouble. You thought you were protecting me from possible incarceration or exile."

"And why are we coming forward now?" It might just work. I would spend the rest of my life ensuring I was worthy of this man's love. Whether I ever loved him back, it didn't matter. I would do it for him.

"We tell them that we decided to come forward because you could already be carrying my child. It's as simple as that." He smiled, his hands lightly caressing me. It was so simple and yet so complex, all in the same breath. Would the Council believe our tale?

Quinten's mouth captured mine, and I let him. It was the least I could do, given he had just promised to put his fate on the line for me. I returned his kiss with as much fervor as possible. He had nice, firm lips and wanted to devour me. I really did walk around with blinders on most of the time, because I'd never seen this coming. Ending the kiss, I scooted away and he tugged my hand.

"Don't move away just yet." He rakishly grinned, a twinkle in his eyes that belied the hunger I sensed in him.

"There's something else we need to do." I maneuvered his seeking hands away. A simple yes from me, and he would have me under him in seconds. He desired me like he desired air to breathe. Why had I never recognized it before? "What's that?" he smirked.

"The Council will likely ask you questions about my"—I considered how to phrase it—"physical form, as someone who's claiming knowledge of it."

I backed fully off the bed and dropped the sheet before I lost my nerve. I held my head high as his startled gaze greedily consumed every ounce of my flesh. His gaze stopped at my breasts and I felt my nipples harden under the scrutiny. His heated stare traveled farther south and stopped at the juncture of my thighs.

"Turn." He choked out, beholding the bounty my body offered like he wanted to pounce but held himself rigidly in check. A part of me wanted him to, but I couldn't so soon after Cade had had his hands on me.

I slowly swiveled until I faced the opposite wall,

and the springs creaked as he left the bed. The air grew thick as I waited. Like a whispered kiss, his hands gingerly stroked my back. My blood hummed with promise. He made me wonder if I had viewed the whole Breeder thing too disparagingly. While there were not any world-altering explosions going off at his touch, this was more than I had ever felt. Then again, maybe there was something fundamentally wrong with me since I failed to get with the program.

His hands cupped my posterior, kneading my backside gently, before they left my body.

"My turn," he said in a deep bedroom voice laced with lust.

I stepped aside and stared as he stripped every ounce of clothing from his body. I had seen him without a shirt plenty of times while we trained, but the rest of him had been a mystery until now. Dark hair covered his finely muscled chest, tapering down over his abdomen before stopping at his staff. The ruby tip bobbed under my scrutiny, and I bit my lip, noticing the glistening drop of moisture on the tip.

Any lingering guilt swimming in my chest about using Quinten for my own gains, to rid myself of Cade before the Council, vanished. He craved me, and not in a "you're a female and we are naked together, so why not?" kind of way. I was a little awed by the depth of his emotions.

"Backside, please," I said, motioning for him to turn around. He winked and did as I requested. Lean, hard muscle covered his back, along with a black tattoo in the form of a wolf's head circled by knot work at the juncture of his neck and shoulders. He had some scarring on his right backside, where a demon's claws had clipped him. I remembered that fight. We had been ambushed, and Quinten had jumped into the skirmish in front of me.

It seemed he had been protecting me all along, and I never noticed. This would work. It had to.

"All right, I think we can both feasibly recount what the other looks like," I murmured, turning away to reestablish safe distance.

His hand slid around my waist and pulled my back against him. His erection strained against my rear, and his mouth laid open kisses along my neck. His tongue traced my birthmark, a dark circle with three vertical lines in the center. Deft fingers glided up and cupped my breasts, pinching the already pert areolas.

"And what do we tell them about our first time?" he purred, nuzzling my neck and almost making me forget that Cade could return to my room at any-time since the sirens were no longer blaring.

"That we were out on a mission six months ago, and one thing led to another. That we have secretly been seeing each other for those six months," I whispered, controlling my voice as his tender ministrations made stirrings of desire gather and throb. His touch filled me with longing, some carnal, some sweet, and I exalted in the hope of more with him.

"How do we explain that you are not with child yet?" he asked with so much optimism in his voice it almost crushed me. He wanted a child? Why had I never known that? Because my world view had consisted only of me, my sins, and my needs. Had I ever stopped to consider what my men wanted?

"We took precautions during intercourse, and you never released your seed inside me." His hips rubbed his erection along the crease in my rear. My fingers threaded through his hair, keeping his head in place so he would continue nibbling right at that spot where my shoulder met my neck.

One of his hands traveled south and dove betwixt my thighs, tangling in my curls. He rubbed my sensitive nub. Hunger speared my body and served as a bucket of ice water over my head.

"Wait," I panted, pulling his hands from my body and removing myself from the circle of his arms. This could not happen like this, not while I still had Cade's stench upon me.

I glanced into his eyes, and the heated desire almost brought me to my knees. Quinten wanted me. His breathing expelled in ragged gasps, his body shuddering in need.

"I'm sorry, but I can't." I hated myself for doing this.

He stepped forward, his hands once more claiming ownership of my body and attempting to pull me close. "But we wouldn't have to fully lie then. We could go before them with you possibly already carrying my child."

Fuck, he was right, but I couldn't yet.

"I can't. Not so soon after Cade …" I explained and glanced down, hoping I convinced him.

"Fine. I understand," he bit out and turned from me, angrily covering his magnificent form. I did the same, not bothering with modesty as I dressed in the first pants and shirt I found. Screw Cade and his orders that I remain naked at all times. After tonight, he would never have a say in my life.

Did Quinten believe this was a dismissal entirely? Panic spiked my blood pressure. I went to him, his body partly turned away from mine. My hands gently clasped his face and brought his gaze to mine. My eyes searched his for any clue to his feelings.

"Please don't be angry. We will … consummate the union. I just can't when I still have that bastard's stench on me. And I want the Council to approve it first. I don't know what I would do if the Council ordered your expulsion to the Desert because of me." I pleaded with him. I meant every word and I watched emotion flicker in his eyes.

His expression softened. His hand cupped my cheek, and he pressed his lips to my forehead. "I understand," he murmured and circled his arms around me.

I allowed it. *Please, gods, let the Council say yes to this union.* Otherwise, I would opt for the Desert.

Sirens blared anew. What the hell? Two sirens in one night? I wished that I had Luke's ability to sense demons farther afield. Their numbers must be massive for the sirens to go off a second time. That meant we needed every soldier out there fighting.

"We should be out there in the combat." I disentangled myself from the comfort his arms granted.

"My orders are to keep you here. And we all know how well your last disobedience went," he chided, hands on his hips. I had never noticed how well he wore his fatigues. It didn't matter as the sirens continued. We were necessary in the field. One extra warrior could make all the difference in battle.

"Yes, but I can't just sit here when our platoons, my platoon is out there fighting for their lives." He must have seen the sense in my argument. He didn't want to be on babysitting duty, even if it would get him laid. Then again, who knew the last time he had been with a woman, so who was I to judge?

"But …" He attempted to argue, ever the levelheaded man, but I caught him glancing at the door, as though he attempted to surmise if our skills were actually necessary.

"Think. When was the last time the sirens went off twice in a row like this? That means our forces need reinforcements like you and me. We can't let them get to the Compound, or worse, inside."

He studied my expression. I witnessed the battle that raged inside him. Consternation settled over his features. He wouldn't let his newest acquisition near a battlefield.

Using every ounce of skill I had, I rubbed my hands up his chest, moving my body intimately against the hard planes of his.

"Please. I couldn't live with myself if we had a chance to save our people and didn't take it. I know I'm not Cantati Forces any-more, but I'm still a soldier and so are you!" I begged, gazing into his eyes, pleading with him to see my point. He stared at my mouth a mere inch from his, and I noticed his eyes fill with unrequited longing. He swallowed, his lips claimed mine for a gentle mating, and I knew I had won.

"Fine. Let's go before I change my mind."

"Thank you." I refrained from dancing a jig at my victory. He could change his mind before we made it out of the Compound. With the sirens continuing their shrill call to arms, I knew this was the right decision. We needed every able-bodied soldier. I had witnessed the difference one person could make on the battlefield.

"We'll stop by my room for weapons," he said.

It was more than I'd hoped for. I hugged him close before I raced to my chest and pulled out a jacket. In demoting me and removing me from Cantati Forces, they had also taken my weapons. More than likely because they were afraid that I would use them on Cade or the Council, not that they were very far off in their estimates. I would make Cade pay for how roughly he'd treated me once the Council reversed their decision, make no mistake.

"I'm ready."

He nodded and gave me a once-over. "Stay close to me, dammit. And don't do anything stupid."

Who, me? Do something stupid? That was all I seemed capable of accomplishing here lately. He wanted assurances that I would be good and not race headlong into trouble. Quinten knew me better than that, so I lied.

"I won't." Although, we both knew that when push came to shove and a battle was underway, a lot of things could go wrong in the space of a heartbeat. The firm line of his mouth told me he didn't buy it, but he accepted my word for now.

"Let's go." With that, we exited my room and headed into the fray.

CHAPTER EIGHT

AFTER A BRIEF stop by Quinten's second-floor room, we scurried out of the Compound. He provided me with a hat in an attempt to shield my face from any guards. It worked. Cantati Forces hurried across the Tower Green, ferrying dispatches from the front, uncaring of other soldiers heading to the front lines in the massive attack.

The majority were heading toward the eastern gate. The ground shook from explosions and the distant din of gunfire. Armed to the teeth, with guards more concerned about not letting the enemy breach our defenses, Quinten and I sneaked out through the western gate unmolested.

The silence on the streets was deafening by comparison. Quinten and I moved wordlessly together. Years of training had honed our ability to work seamlessly. We ran in tandem, with Quinten on point.

We covered ground quickly, traveling in the direction of gunshots. Sounds of battle increased with every block we passed. A mile from the wall, we crossed over the threshold of hell. Cade's platoon and at least half of mine were engaged in ferocious combat.

I didn't spy my majors. Ben, Nick, and Luke were not part of the melee that I could see. Relief washed through me. I prayed they had been assigned to the Compound with my absence.

Entering the battle, Quinten and I worked together, forming a shield, using the other to protect our backs. My sensors were on high alert.

Three Feronte demons bent on ripping me to shreds crashed through a broken line of defense to reach me. With heads shaped like dragons, they had retractable claws on each of their forearms, but their fireballs were the most deadly. They could shoot those suckers up to twenty-five feet and had near-perfect aim. My blade slashed, and I flayed the first two demons into pieces.

Screeching, the remaining Feronte growled.

I blocked its heavy, clawed fists. Then I danced precipitously out of arm's reach when two more Ferontes emerged from the hoopla. How many more were there? The number of demons were staggering. My demon-detecting powers were on overdrive, flooded by their energy. I had to block it, shore up my psychic shields, otherwise this many would undermine my ability to defend myself and anyone else.

Quinten had engaged with a group of Hatha,

careful of their six-inch retractable claws. Those suckers hurt like hell when they gouged flesh and carried a venom that, if left untreated, wreaked havoc on the human body.

I ducked and swiveled, arcing my blade against a Feronte's throat.

Two Efrits joined the fight. I hated Efrits. I dropped my blade, switching to my Glock .45. Big bastards like these needed big bullets. My finger relaxed against the trigger.

The Efrits' bodies coiled, milliseconds from action. My finger depressed the trigger. I emptied a clip into those two. Damn near cut one in half. I dodged a fire blast from another Feronte, dived and rolled, reloading my handgun with a full clip. Gravel skinned my knees. On my side, I aimed, squeezed the trigger. The Feronte crashed to the ground.

I heard a Toth's heavy footfalls as it charged. Its three heads shaped like a velociraptor's, and on each head they had a mouth filled with wickedly long fangs. Damn thing openly hissing as it stalked me. These suckers were massive barrel chested brutes. In seconds I had the Glock back in its holster and swiveled my focus. Back on my feet, I whipped the blade in an arc, sliced it through bone and sinew removing all three heads before they could sample my flesh. Sounds of the battle seared my ears. I couldn't tell who was winning, us or them. Best we could do was keep demons from each other's backs. Any demon foolish enough to charge Quinten or me was crow fodder.

A machine built for killing, I hacked and slashed at every tentacle, claw, and tusk. Body parts littered the ground. Blood ran in rivulets and stained the street. And through it all, I listened to the sounds of battle around me.

Mammoth hands snatched me from behind, slamming my body against the nearest wall and stealing my breath. My blade clanked at my feet.

"What the fuck are you doing here?" Cade snarled mere inches from my face as he restrained my arms, keeping them from my firearm.

"Saving your collective asses, apparently," I remarked, aching for my gun or blade.

"You are not Cantati Forces any longer." His warm breath washed over my face and made me gag. We were at war, and he worried more about his prize than his men. Some leader he had become. The general needed to know about his weakness.

"Let go of her," Quinten demanded.

Damn him, he'd promised he wouldn't engage Cade. If I had not been seeing stars from the impact with the wall, I would have given him a piece of my mind. It would have been far easier to bash their heads together. They both had forgotten the full-scale battle happening around us.

"Or what?" Cade tossed over his shoulder. The certainty in his smug response sickened me. Like he believed himself to be the top dog, and no one would argue against him. Wouldn't he be surprised when Quinten and I went before the Council?

"I'll make you," Quinten replied, all puffed-up proud, while I struggled to breathe against Cade's tight grip around on my throat.

"Yeah, you and what army?" Cade smirked. I wanted to wipe the smugness off his face. If I could only reach my gun, I would take care of Cade. Then Quinten and I would have ourselves a little chat.

Quinten yanked Cade's grasp on my throat. I slumped against the wall rubbing my bruised throat, as Cade rounded on Quinten with his fists.

Horror filled me when Cade rushed Quinten. But he was ready for him. The blows they landed would have made lesser men crumble. It should have made me feel girly and feminine at their chest beating over me. It didn't. I wanted to jump between them and stop the madness. I pulled my gun and retrieved my blade.

"I'll see you in the brig for this, Major," Cade barked, while throwing a punch aimed at Quinten's jaw. Quinten dodged Cade's fist.

"She's mine, Cade. Has been for a while. In fact, she's likely already carrying my child. The Council will reverse their decision. Touch her again and I'll kill you." Quinten had a few devices up his sleeve and countered Cade's assault with a few solid blows of his own.

Enraged, Cade unleashed the berserker within

and pushed Quinten into a defensive attack. Demons swarmed, and I became engaged with the nearest Yathuri.

All around, men and demons fought. Men died. Demons died. The sounds of the battle diminished, and I glanced around after beheading a Hatha. Cade had Quinten in a dead-lock grip around his neck.

Sorrow filled Quinten's eyes as he fought against Cade's hold.

"Let him go, Cade," I shouted. "Enough. You made your point."

Cade glanced at me, and I was not certain what he saw. Maybe it was my defiance of his orders. Maybe a part of him sensed that he would never get the chance to claim me and that Quinten threatened his possession of me. Quinten's face turned red from suffocation. He bucked and fought Cade's unflinching, unyielding grip. The dead forces at work inside Cade shuttered his expression as he grasped Quinten's head.

With a swiftness that stole my breath, Cade snapped Quinten's neck, the crack of bone sounding hollow in the lifeless space, and I watched my salvation fall. His sightless eyes, the ones that had glanced at me in adoration and hunger a short while ago, stared lifelessly back at me. His strong body, full of compact muscles, collapsed to the ground.

Dead. Quinten was dead.

"NOOOOOO!" I screamed.

I went after Cade. My throat bunched up tight

with unshed emotion. I may not have loved Quinten, but I had cared for him, and this monster had taken him from me. The big moments like this stole all rational thought from my body. As a woman who had been dubbed the Ice Maiden, I was all emotions and rage. I was just better at hiding them than most people. I felt things so deeply. My surface might appear to be a calm lake, but my emotions were more bottomless than any ocean, with turbulent currents that dragged the unwary into the abyss.

A vehemence I rarely unleashed took hold and filled my soul with the ice I had been accused of for so long. I lifted my Glock, sighted it, and fired my last bullet into Cade's chest. Utter shock registered on his features as he glanced at the blood blooming upon his chest. For Quinten, and for me. He would never violate anyone again. Cade toppled backward, dead before his body impacted the ground.

I glanced around the field of battle. There was no one else. They were all dead.

CHAPTER NINE

I OPENED MY shields, expanding my energy outward until I sat in the epicenter. Nothing. No life signatures except mine. The Compound was far enough away that the people there did not trigger my sensors.

I knelt next to Quinten. Gently, with as much care as possible, I closed his sightless eyes. I stared at his handsome face. My fingers trailed over his cheeks. Anguish stole my breath as I gazed at his prone form. I may not have been in love with him, but he was my friend. One I had trusted implacably. I clasped his lifeless hand, devoid of all the solid strength I had come to expect. I would miss his warm smile, calm demeanor, and the possibility of an us.

Wetness splashed on my hands and I realized I was crying. The hope his feelings had awakened was crushed under the oppressive weight of his demise. I would carry him back. I owed him that much. He deserved a warrior's funeral.

Hundreds of bodies lay strewn about me. Demons

hugged by the human counterparts who killed them, embracing each other for all eternity in death.

I had to dispose of all the corpses. But first, I spent the next hour filching supplies from the dead. Had to, as morbid as it might seem. We needed the weapons too badly. The pile beside Quinten's body grew. I'd have to send a detail company back for these with a cart. Once I had remanded all the available weapons into two piles next to Quinten, I began setting the bodies on fire, starting at the far end of the battleground from Quinten's body. Humans intermixed with demons were easy. Demon bodies did not need a burning agent to ignite, partially due to their sulfuric compound, but hot enough to help incinerate the human bodies amidst them. I memorized the face of every one of my men who had perished. I should be numb to it all, but I wasn't. How could anyone not feel the senselessness of it all?

How had this attack happened? Why had Drystan caught us so unprepared, as though we continued to forget that he wanted the extinction of the human race, to breed more of his demons and claim Earth as his dominion? This had been the largest skirmish in months. At least a hundred men were dead. Including Quinten. There had to be hundreds of demons. I'd never get an accurate count with all the body parts.

I ventured from body pile to body pile with the flame thrower I'd discovered on one of the deceased. We had been so vastly outnumbered in this fight. I reached Cade's body, his face forever frozen with the shock of his death. It had been a nicer end than what he had deserved. I did not regret it. The Council would kill me for my actions, if they found out. I ended a man's life, an offense punishable by death. Regardless of my reasons for doing so, in light of my recent defiance of their missives, the Council could never know. I set the flame to his clothing, watching as the flames licked his body until it engulfed him. There was nothing more I could do for any of them. My tears were empty, and sorrow burned into anger. I would hold to the promise I had made, the one to my mother, that I would rid the Earth of demons. I would. That was why I was here, to end Drystan and all his demon minions until this planet was wiped clean of their foul existence.

The Council would listen to reason with the latest losses. They must. Otherwise, they precipitated our doom. I did not regret ending Cade's sorry existence. The Council preached that every life was precious and must be protected. But he had lost his objectivity and murdered Quinten without a second thought. How many more men had died at his hands when he deemed them unnecessary?

It was past time I returned to the Compound. Had they breached our walls and entered Command? Or had the Red Squadron beat them back and held our defensive line? I hoisted Quinten's body over my shoulder, thanking the gods for my powers. If I had merely been human, I would never have been able to carry his two hundred pounds of dead weight. I shot my sensors out, searching for any demon signatures. Satisfied there wasn't a bleep on my radar, I high-tailed it, as fast as I could with my burden, away from the carnage, leaving behind the weapons, erasing my energy tracers as I went, cleaning up any trail a demon might find. The general had taught me, although all Cantati were trained with the knowledge. The best way to describe it was, we took our energy, expanded it outside ourselves, and used it like a washrag to remove any trace amounts of our energy.

I did not understand the physics behind it, but knew it had something to do with a Cantati's powers. It was something we were gifted with, like SPD, or Synaptic Pathways Diversion. Part of being one of the enlightened, as the Coven had nicknamed us.

We could move and work with the elements of nature. I thought it was nature's way of trying to balance the scales, and keep humans from extinction. Granted, we weren't really human, not entirely anyway, our genetic make-up different from that of our human brethren.

Block by block, I swept the area of my signature and that of any Cantati that could lead the enemy back to the Compound. Sweat dripped, coating my skin, even in the cool brisk temperatures of a London fall night. The extra weight of Quinten's body made this task much more difficult.

I arrived back at the Compound in a little under an hour. As I strode through the western gate, a group of soldiers took Quinten's body for me.

"We'll take him from here, sir."

"Thank you, Private." His body would be prepared for its funeral pyre. We used the Tower Bridge and Thames River as our burial ground. The body burned on top of a funeral pyre, then its ashes were scattered into the water below.

I marched toward the Command Center. The general needed to know how many losses we had sustained. Then we must shore up resources and prepare for the next attack. He had to rethink his worldwide assault strategy with the severity of this recent annihilation.

The halls were crowded with refugees and soldiers alike. The whole Compound was suffused in chaos. Women sobbed, children cried, and men wore haggard, shell-shocked expressions. What the hell had happened while I was gone?

I spotted Ben and Luke over the ruckus. I approached them just as they noticed me. They were at my side in a heartbeat. Relief riddled their faces. Ben reached me first and pulled me into a bear hug. He squeezed me tight before releasing me.

"Lieutenant. We thought you were dead," Ben admonished, and I caught the glimmer of wetness in his eyes.

"Where were you?" Luke asked reproachfully. My

golden boy, always so adroit, brought me up short with his question. He knew something. They all would once the patrols spotted the fires.

"Out with the Blue Squad," I replied, hating myself. Quinten had died because I had convinced him we were needed in the field. Maybe we had been and had beaten back monsters who would have reached the Compound. Or maybe we had caused more deaths, those of our now-fallen brethren, because of our actions.

"Where is the Blue Squad?" Luke inquired.

I brought my glance up to his. His gaze hardened with what he saw there. He knew. But he waited, needing to hear it from my lips.

"Dead," I answered. Luke cringed away from me, as though I had scalded him with my words and betrayed an unspeakable, invisible bond between us. With a swiftness that stunned me, he severed his kinder feelings toward me, the camaraderie we had always shared. In a millisecond, they evaporated.

"Quinten?" Ben cried. I winced. They had been friends for a long time. His death was the hardest to report.

I shook my head. How would they react when they discovered it was my fault? That my decision, my selfishness, had caused his demise. I had irrevocably altered his fate and my own. All because I could not get with the program and breed with Cade.

Ben hung his head but not before I noticed the sheen of unshed tears.

"Come, the general has been looking for you." He said with a coldness I had not known he had in him. His golden-boy image had hardened into a disdainful god. He understood, more than Ben, that I had been involved with our friend's death. He blamed me for it. I did, too. There would be no absolution for this night. There would be no more chances from the Council or from the men I had once called friends, if they ever discovered my horrible secret. I was an abomination to the Cantati way of life, and I would pay for my recklessness.

I followed Luke and Ben into the Command Center. My father saw me the moment I crossed the threshold.

"Put her in my office. Guard the door to make sure she doesn't leave," he ordered. "Yes, sir." Luke saluted and grabbed my arm. Ben opened the door and Luke dragged me into my father's dimly lit office.

Guard me? Was I under arrest? Did they know the crimes I'd committed?

"Stay." He pointed before he and Ben departed.

Exhaustion settled in. I had been living on nothing but anger for what seemed like days, but no more than thirty-six hours had passed since the Council's initial ruling. How had it all come to this?

I sat in my father's chair, uncaring of the blood

caked on my clothing. Leaning my head back, I started to nod off, until the office door slammed open. My father stood at attention, his glance scathing where there should have been concern and relief.

"What the hell happened, Lieutenant? You were relieved of your duties and expressly ordered to remain in your room. So why is it, when I sent soldiers to retrieve you and bring you into Command, that you were nowhere to be found? Then you appear, hours later, covered in blood. Explain."

He stood, a soldier stoically at attention, awaiting my response. Had I always been a disappointment to him? Were we forever destined to disagree and butt heads?

"They are all dead."

"What? Where did you get your intel?"

"I went with Cade and Quinten, to help them, but they all died," I lied. He didn't need to know my part in it.

"Cade's platoon?"

"All dead. I'm surprised the scouts haven't seen the fires I set. We need to send a small unit to retrieve all the weapons I gathered from the dead in Sector Four."

"Christ." He rubbed his hands over his face. "I'll be right back. Stay here. I'll have someone bring you some food."

Dad exited his office. I noticed Ben and Luke were still stationed outside his door. I heard the deep rumble of my dad's voice as he issued orders for the weapons detail. I collapsed back onto his chair and waited.

I heard movement around outside his office. Time crept by, and voices whispered outside the door. A thousand weights bore down upon my soul. Images of Quinten and the guys laughing together in the mess hall, playing poker in the barracks, and even my first full glimpse of his nude form. Those pictures, the memories, especially the last glimpse, his sorrow when he realized he would lose the fight and we would never be, pummeled me.

Someone brought me food, a Levare woman, whom Ben and Luke allowed into the general's office. She shuffled over to the desk and laid a tray down with today's gruel. "Thank you," I murmured, while Luke glared daggers in my direction. He could piss off. I knew he was angry at all the deaths, but it was his shoddy intel that the general would have looked to when issuing orders. The woman nodded her head and retraced her steps.

Luke slammed the door after she exited the room. I had expected the cold shoulder, the distancing from my father, but I had never expected it from Luke. Just when I thought I couldn't feel worse, that my soul could not bleed any further, I was proved wrong.

I leaned my head back against the chair. Avoiding the gruel, which smelled like spoiled fish, I closed my eyes.

The door shuddered open on its hinges and slammed into the wall.

"Dammit, girl!" Dad shut the door behind him and stomped into the room. "You were right. Every last bleeding one of those men, gone. What the fuck happened? And why were you with them?"

Exhaustion had dulled the edges some, but I had to lie. No one could know my true crimes against my people.

"We were ambushed by hundreds, General. Your initial reports were wrong about the numbers. I fear Drystan has figured out we have someone who can sense his numbers. When the sirens went off for a second time, Quinten and I joined Cade's bunch. They were already overrun by the time we joined. We were needed, General, and I believe we prevented them from breaching our walls."

"Bleeding Christ, this is a mess."

"You need me back leading the Cantati Forces, not as a Breeder. I think the worldwide attacks need to be changed or postponed until we can figure out Drystan's next move."

I glanced at him. I needed to be reinstated, to fight back so that Quinten did not die in vain. The only way I could ensure that was out in the field.

"Agreed. Listen to me." He leaned in close. "There may be a way around the Council's orders. They won't allow it unless you pick another, right this moment, and we tell the Council."

"Like hell!" No, I wasn't doing it. I could still smell Quinten. The last thing I wanted was another man in my bed. Or worse, dead because of me.

"It will be a farce. We'll get one of your men to agree, but he won't actually bed you. Understand? Then I will petition the Council that until I can find another candidate, you will be leading what is left of the Green Squad until you are pregnant."

Could I pick another and lie to the Council? At least with Quinten I had been willing to offer him my body so it would not have been a complete lie. Who did I have left to choose from? Luke, Ben, or Nick? Picking another would never assuage my guilt over Quinten. If I had to pick between the remaining candidates, it would have to be Luke. Ben had shit for brains at times, and Nick was far too young.

This did not sit well with me. "But what happens when I don't end up pregnant?"

"We'll deal with that when the time comes. Will you do it?" Dad kept glancing at his computer screens, like he was just as worried about committing treason as I was.

Could I do this? I would have my life back, but I would be damning someone else. I had to. The stakes were too high, and we had lost too many good men today. If this was the sure fire way to put me back in field command, so be it.

"Fine, I'll do it." There were moments that define someone. Moments when faced with the surety of defeat, we catch a glimmer of hope that one could survive living.

"Who?" He was curious and showed more interest in me than he had in a decade. Would wonders never cease to amaze me? It had taken him believing he had lost me to show that he cared.

"Luke."

My father actually smiled. "Good girl."

He went to his door. "Luke, could you come in here please?"

"Yes, sir." Luke did the general's bidding without question. He shut the door behind himself and approached my father's desk, saluting.

"Sir, I apologize that the numbers I read were incorrect. Sector radar had not detected those numbers, either. If you want to remove me from duty, I understand."

"Have a seat, Major. I don't believe you intentionally gave us the wrong numbers. I think Alana is right. Drystan has found a way to block your abilities, or cloud them at the very least. That's not why I brought you in here."

Surprised, Luke glanced between me and my father. "Then ..."

"With Cade's entire division gone, along with part of the Green Squad, I need Alana back commanding Cantati Forces. The only way I can convince the Council is if she already has another mate in place."

Luke appeared shell-shocked, "And you want me to be her chosen mate?"

"On paper, yes. Alana belongs in the field, leading my men, not as a Breeder. You won't actually consummate your union, at least not initially. We need time to rebuild our ranks, while keeping this place safe. For all her rebelliousness, she's the best leader I have, and if we are to survive, we need her skills."

Warmth seeped through me, and I hid my smile.

Luke shot me a derisive look. "And you are okay with deceiving the Council like this?"

"Yes. Are you? With Cade's death, I have to choose another mate, even if it is a fake mate."

"I need to think about it." Luke's agitation burst out. He stood and left without being dismissed.

My father studied me. He would forgive Luke his lack of protocol. We had dropped a bomb on him and asked him to betray his oath. I'd caused one hell of a ruckus when I was assigned to Cade. Luke deserved the same consideration. Although, being on the receiving end of Luke's consternation made me feel like I was a three-headed monster.

"We still have to face the Council. Do you think Luke will come around?"

"Honestly, I don't know." I shook my head. "Wait, didn't the Council leave for the Versailles Compound?"

"Yes." He hit the controls on his computer, and the holograms bloomed.

"Come in, Coven Mother."

The images of the Council appeared on the screens. The Coven Mother stared me down, boring holes into my soul before shifting her focus to my father.

"What about the rest of Cade's men, General? The missive we received only spoke of his ill fate." I had been removed from under the razor's edge of scrutiny for the moment.

"Dead," The general uttered.

The Council members cried out.

"And you, you were part of this?" the Coven Mother inquired, glowering at me. "Why did you defy the Council again, Alana? You have consistently challenged our orders. And now your chosen mate perished in the attack."

"Hear her out, Amelia," my father interjected.

"Silence, Commander. You will not interfere with these proceedings again or I will have you removed from command. Understood?" Amelia glared at my father and I noticed hatred in her eyes. In all my years, I had never heard anyone speak down to my father or belittle his station.

"Yes, ma'am," he replied, and I heard him grind his teeth. So apparently theirs was not a match made in heaven. Maybe that was why he was willing to help me now.

"What actually happened out there? How is it you survived when no one else did?" Amelia asked. She wanted to use magic on me to uncover the truth.

I could tell she desired it greatly, but the rest of the Council would find it appalling. She was a bleeding hypocrite.

"Council members, had I not defied the will of the Council by joining the battle, the Compound walls would have been breached. They attacked us with hundreds of their kind."

"How do I know you are not lying to us?"

"You don't. What I do know is that I made a difference today and stopped their forward progression. Punish me, if you like, but I was doing this for our people, to protect them. You might want to consider doing the same."

Council members gasped. My father shook his head at my response. Screw that.

"I request that I be reinstated in the Cantati Forces."

"We need you as a Breeder," came Amelia's scathing reply, like that was all I should expect from my life and should be thankful for it.

"Council members, I can be both. I am needed on the force, but will also concede after the good men we lost today that we do need to replenish our ranks and will serve until such time as I am with child. I will only leave the forces long enough to birth the child, then return to active duty."

"I agree, Amelia," my father said. "I need the lieutenant reinstated. I don't have anyone else as qualified to lead the forces. Right now we are sitting ducks with our losses."

The Coven Mother glanced between us. She was not happy about the direction these proceedings had taken. The other members whispered amongst themselves until the Coven Mother glared at them sharply. It struck me between the eyes. Power, I had it, and that threatened Amelia. She liked her position, the accolades and the authority it granted her, too much.

"And did you make your choice?"

"Yes." Luke would forgive me, eventually. Once the dust settled a bit, we could even discuss the potential future in which we could make it a real union. But for now, the sake of our people must come first.

"Who?" Amelia asked, her hard face showing a bare shimmer of curiosity.

Forgive me, Quinten. I promise not to forget your sacrifice.

"Luke Holland," I declared.

"So be it. You are reinstated as lieutenant until such time as you are carrying the offspring of Major Holland." Amelia ruled in my favor, for once. I think the rest of the Council would have rebuked her had she tried to keep me from the front lines. The Council was afraid, as they should be, that Drystan was winning with his new combat strategies.

"Thank you." It was more than I'd hoped could happen. For whatever reasons, my fate had become intertwined with Luke. I prayed he would keep our secret.

"Fine. You are dismissed." Amelia shifted her attention from me to my father. He nodded that I could leave his office.

As I walked toward the door, I knew Quinten's death had changed everything. Once again my fate had been tossed upon another path and I did not know whether to rejoice or cry.

May the gods protect me.

If they were even listening . . .

How had it come to this?

CHAPTER TEN

OUTSIDE, LUKE AND Ben were stationed near the general's office door. They stood at attention as I closed the door behind me. Luke avoided eye contact with me. But they both saluted.

"Lieutenant, your orders?" Ben asked, his normal jovial grin replaced by grim determination. I wanted to comfort him. He and Quinten had been real tight. They had gone through training together and had even been roommates. A lot of soldiers were forced to share rooms. With the overcrowding from citizens, there was nowhere else for us to put them.

I saluted them back.

"Ben, I want you to go to the armory and do a complete weapons inventory. Take Nick and if you need to, get Declan and Jared to assist. We need to know what our supplies look like."

"Yes, sir." He replied, heading off to the armory.

"Luke, walk with me." I glanced at him, searching for the man I knew hidden by the current gruff exterior. He mourned Quinten. We all did. It was more though. He acted like I had betrayed him somehow. By the gods, men were more emotional creatures than women.

We needed to discuss the Council's ruling. Although, his demeanor made me think that, unlike Quinten, or hell even Cade, he would not be pleased by the news.

"After you, Lieutenant." Luke gestured for me to proceed. The moment we were out of hearing range of the Command Center, he let loose. "What the hell happened out there? I knew Quinten, and even he wouldn't have disobeyed a direct order unless he had been coerced."

Luke was right, Quinten never would have disobeyed a direct order, not without provocation. With my back to Luke, I closed my eyes, took a deep breath, and gave him as much of the truth as I was willing to share. He couldn't ever know the full extent I had played in Quinten's demise. Cade wasn't the only one with a cell waiting for him in hell. I had a nice one of my very own reserved.

"He went because I ordered him to," I confessed. A tear slipped down my cheek. I had thought I had used up all my tears. I swiped it from my cheek before he noticed it.

"Why would he do that?" I felt Luke hovering behind me. If I were given to fanciful musings, I'd say he wanted to shake the answers out of me.

What could I say? That he had wanted me for years and I used him to get out of a bad situation? That I persuaded him to follow me into hell, and he went willingly to his doom? I would carry that guilt with me all the days of my life, regardless of how short or long it may be.

"When the sirens went off a second time, Quinten and I knew it was bad. We made a difference out there. He made a difference. But he was out-maneuvered, and I couldn't get to him fast enough." I swallowed, attempting to moisten my dry throat. That much was true at least. Cade had out-gunned him.

"Do you really believe that?" He dragged me into my room and crossed his arms over his chest. The muscles in his arms flexed. I focused on those muscles instead of the condemnation glaring in his face. Then it hit me. My gaze shot up and I glanced in Luke's eyes. He wasn't really angry with me, it was just a mask that covered the guilt that was eating him alive. He believed this attack, and all the losses were his fault.

"We needed every soldier in that fight. I have made some bad choices in my time, I won't deny that. But this wasn't one of them. If we hadn't gone, then the Compound would have been breached. I'm sorry that your powers have been compromised by Drystan. Quinten's death was not your fault. None of them were, do you hear me? You didn't know. None of us did."

Luke turned away and punched the wall. He pounded his fist repeatedly in the same spot and blood bloomed on the white wall. I grabbed his arm before he could smash his fist against the wall again. He shot me a ferocious look as I restrained his arm, his blue eyes cloudy with his turbulent emotions. I slid my arms around him and embraced him.

Luke and I had never really touched in anything more than a plutonic way. He stood stiffly, as though he held himself together like a tightly wound watch. I stood fast, holding him close. A breath shuddered from deep within him, and his arms enveloped me, pulling me tightly against him as the dam of his emotions burst free.

I held him as the storm of his emotions battered him. Smoothing my hands across his back, I soothed him as best I could. Standing inside the circle of his arms, I allowed some of my own grief to subside. In our world, life was short and brutal. It was rarer still, to find solace in the starkness of our lives. And in this moment, I accepted the comfort he returned. I waited for Luke to withdraw before moving away.

"Better?" I asked, rubbing his arms.

"Yes. Thanks." He replied, the sorrow remained but was no longer drowning him.

I spied blood welling and seeping from his

swollen knuckles. I hoped like hell he hadn't broken them in his fury. "Let me clean you up. Come on."

I went into my bathroom, expecting him to follow. He did. I grabbed my medicine kit from under the stainless steel sink. Setting it on the small steel shelf, I turned to him. The restricted confines of my tiny bathroom were more pronounced with his six-two frame standing within it.

"Did the Council reinstate you?" he asked.

"Yes, they did." I clasped his injured hand, rinsing the blood from his knuckles. Unsure of his reaction, I continued hesitantly, "The Council has also made you my mate."

"They did, huh? And you and the general had nothing to do with that?" He replied sardonically.

"Look, Luke, we're friends. I'm sorry that I put you in this position, that the general asked this of you. The Council asked me, and I chose you. I'd rather it be someone I actually like. I'm sorry if this is not what you want. It only has to be a farce to keep me in command."

Luke studied me, a light in his eyes different from anything I had ever seen. Did he desire a union between us?

"Say something," I pleaded with him as I wrapped his hand.

"Yes, I'll do it. On one condition," he stepped forward, closing the gap between us. My breath caught. I put my hands up to keep some distance between us, and my hands met his solidly muscled chest.

"What?" He almost seemed like the Luke I knew, but more confident in his footing with me.

"That our union not be a farce. That we are mated to each other in fact as well as deed." He sounded pretty pleased with himself.

Great mother goddess!

"Luke, I ..." I wasn't ready. My emotions had been through a whirlpool in the last few days, and I hardly knew what direction was up.

"That's the condition or I walk and inform the Council. I will be here after patrol and we can begin," he bluntly stated. Son of a bitch was blackmailing me, and he knew it. He had me over a barrel and whether I wanted it or not, he was stealing my choice. I deserved it, I guessed, since I had done the same to him with the Council.

I was out of options. In order to help our people, I needed to be in the field. If the way to do so was to be mated to Luke in truth, then so be it. I could imagine worse fates. "We can begin after our patrol."

"Really? You're sure?" He studied me for any hint of discord.

"Yes." I assured him. For better or worse, we were mates. I slid my body closer and watched his pupils dilate, darkening to midnight. I noticed the tick in his jaw, and the pulse in his neck thumped. He wanted me that much was certain. My emotions were too much of a jumbled mess to feel anything more than relief. I was back where I belonged, in command of my squad.

"Good." He pulled me close, with the hint of a smile on his face.

The ground rumbled and shook.

Sirens blared.

Sweet merciful goddess!

Luke and I stared at each other. Our interchange momentarily suspended. A noxious mix of smoke, gunpowder, and sulfur began to fill the room. I heard screams.

Another attack? So close to the last one? What the hell?

"We need to go." I maneuvered out of Luke's arms, pushing past him out of the bathroom. From the sounds of it, the Cantati needed every soldier out fighting Drystan's forces.

"Stay, until we know more. For me, please," he asked. I was his superior officer, regardless of the fact that we were mates in the eyes of the Council. The thought of hiding in my room while the rest of humanity battled for survival riled my blood. My squad needed me more than I needed to assuage his ownership of me.

"Not gonna happen, major. I need you with me on this. Let's go." I would not stay locked in my room like a Breeder. Another ground shattering rumble boomed, rattling even my teeth. There would be time to argue the finer points of this relationship later. Right now, we had to join the fight.

I grabbed my gun. Luke begrudgingly nodded his agreement and we raced into storm.

-The End-

ANOINTED

BY MAGGIE MAE GALLAGHER

****

My name is Alana Devereaux. I enjoy the simple things in life, walks in the park, sky gazing, and ripping a demon's heart out through its chest. I am a demon slayer, the last of my kind, and I have been sent back through time to save your world. How am I doing so far? My time travel went haywire, all the signs I needed to stop the prophecy have passed, and the only way I can save my world is by keeping yours from ending. Then there's Gaelen, most days I want to deck him. He hides his true motives and if it was not for the intel he had, I would be rid of him. Any day in my life without a demon attack is a good day; I haven't had a whole lot of those lately. The only problem is, if I don't stop the Mutari, this world will burn.

Enjoy the following excerpt from

ANOINTED …

****

YEAR 83 AFTER MUTARI

Bloody hell! The Coven's barriers had failed.

"Get to the Command Center," I shouted at Luke, Ben and Nick as I passed, my voice drowned out by screeching air raid sirens.

Demons? Inside the compound? They were an incessant wave bent on destroying every man, woman, and child who crossed their path. How the hell did they get in? The Densare Council had never experienced a breach of this magnitude.

Ben and Luke shouldered past me with their guns drawn, Nick a heartbeat behind. Men pretended women were good for nothing but the continuation of the species. They were our protectors in every fight, but I was better than any man and they knew it. Lights flickered sporadically, the fluorescent bulbs sputtering a few seconds before total darkness descended. Demons cut the power grid. The new cross-breed bastards were smarter than the average hell's spawn.

Red hazards stuttered on as the generator kicked into gear. Emergency lights buzzed. I lost sight of the guys ahead as the glow bounced off concrete gray walls in a mismatched fashion creating pockets of total darkness.

The command center seemed miles away. Already sprinting full out, I pushed my legs harder. My muscles strained under the brutal treatment.

The ground buckled. Chunks of concrete sprayed skyward. Shielding my face with my hands, my feet lost their purchase and I stumbled into the wall.

Son of a bitch, were they using grenades? Smoke billowed in the halls. A suffocating mixture of sulfur and gun powder penetrated my lungs. My eyes burned, blinded by smoke so thick it muted the glow of the hazard lights.

How would demons obtain grenades, for God's sake? Demons weren't braincases. What new horror had they unleashed on humanity? Was it not enough that our numbers decreased every day?

My gun drawn, I raced around the next blind corner. The pop of rapid gunfire exploded. The tink, tink, tink of shell casings from Ben's forty caliber made me smile. He loved that gun. The reverberation echoed throughout the corridors.

A horde of Hathas, big grey, eight-foot monstrosities with lethal strength, advanced on the line of soldiers. Drystan's foot soldiers were waylaying our men, two and three at a time. The tight quarters outside the Command Center made it difficult to maneuver.

I had to reach the Command Center. We were being overrun ... fast.

One by one, every gun was silenced. Horrified screams shattered the stillness. I recognized three bloodcurdling moans: Ben, Nick, and Luke were dying. The demons were hungry, their sharp tusks now bathed in blood. I shuddered. It was not the way I wanted to die.

Soldiers positioned at the center door used flame throwers to rain fire upon the demon mass approaching. I darted along the wall, ever at the ready to empty my clip into a demon. Burnt flesh heavily scented with sulfur smothered my senses as I charged around the last corner. My father, General Casey O'Hara, shouted the order to seal the center doors.

May the gods help all those left outside.

Declan and Jared shoved them closed as I slid across the threshold. The doors were made of concrete and reinforced steel. Once sealed, nothing could get in or out.

The Cantati were losing this fight. We sorely needed a plan. The attack seemed organized. Their formations sent my sensors into overdrive. Who led them? Or better yet, why had they been unleashed? This assault was different from the rest. The certainty of it resonated in my bones.

Jared and Declan strained with a heavy metal black cabinet that stood taller than either man. Metal scraped concrete as they positioned it up against the door. Could the Hathas get through? There had been a smattering of cross-breeds in the group—those half demon, half human abominations were like rabid dogs on steroids.

After my last mission, it was better that we were all fully armed and prepared than caught with our pants down. "Colin, open the weapons chest and make sure everyone is fully armed, got it?" I ordered the freckle-faced kid, barely old enough to shave, on my right as I gasped oxygen into my lungs. My pulse pounded from my mad dash. A few years in the field and his skin wouldn't be so unblemished—if he made it a few years. Had I ever been that green? At twenty-three, compared to him, I was ancient.

"Yes, Lieutenant. Right away, ma'am," Colin replied with something akin to reverence. At least he recognized the chain of command, even with some-one who was *persona non grata* at the moment.

"Alana, my office. Now," General O'Hara demanded. Cantati forces taking up positions near the center door glanced back at his harsh command.

Well shit, that took a lot longer than I thought it would.

When he gave a command, you followed it or he relieved you. His voice stirred, leaving traces of apprehension along my spine.

"But … sir?" I cringed inwardly. Glancing at his tall, sturdy frame, always dressed in camo military garb, I admitted he had every right to be pissed. My hands balled into fists. At a time like this, what the hell had gotten into him? We needed to form a counter offensive, not discuss the varied details of my recent failure. If we survived this assault, we could examine the fact that an entire Cantati squad was nothing more than demon fodder because of me. The images from that mission had been emblazoned upon my soul. I shoved it from my mind because if I allowed it, the guilt would swallow me whole.

Barking his response in short, clipped words, he bellowed. "No time, damn it! My office, NOW!" He stiffly turned, expecting me to follow. Snarling a command over his shoulder he shouted, "Keep that door closed. Don't let those bastards in."

Bloody hell, like I didn't have enough problems with these guys. They'd talk about my sparring with the General for weeks. Dread churned my belly. I ignored the dozen pair of eyes that studied my reaction, me the fabled ice queen who'd led good men to their deaths. They all blamed me. Head held high, unwilling to falter beneath their steely gazes, I followed him and focused on his bald head instead of their glares. As I walked past the blinking computer lights and sector radar, I shot a quick glance at the map and my blood chilled. I marched past the radar into Dad's office. He'd bark, but he knew I was the best he had.

Dad typed a code into his computer with enough force I thought the keyboard buttons would fall off from the reverberation. The wall behind his desk moved, sliding open to reveal a hidden room.

Bloody hell.

There was a vault in Dad's office? It was small, not much larger than a walk-in closet, the inside walls lined with silver metal compartments, each locked with a security keypad. He stepped to the far left corner, keyed in a second code, and had his thumb print scanned. A hatch opened seamlessly, emitting a luminescent violet light. He removed two items from the vault, a glowing jade orb the size of my hand and a leather-bound manuscript.

The vault door closed upon his exit. Dad sat across from me at his desk. I'd always thought of his heavy, old-world, wooden desk as Dad's one concession to history. His lips tensed into a flat, compressed line; his eyes searched mine. Fingers of dread reached up, grabbed ahold of my windpipe and squeezed. I didn't want to hear what he was about to say.

Sorrow flitted through his brown gaze for a split second. A shock-wave rumbled through the compound and the resounding boom from another grenade rent the air. "Your orders are to travel back and stop the Mutari."

"What?" I croaked. He wanted me to stop the Mutari? It was the single biggest event to ever happen to mankind. Eighty years ago by our best estimate, Drystan, ruler of Infernus, breached the walls between his realm and ours, unleashing his demon armies upon humanity. Billions of humans died within the first twenty-four hours of the assault. He wanted me to stop that?

No way.

Shaking my head, I was sure I heard him wrong. Could he actually send me to another time? Time travel wasn't possible, was it?

"This Moldevian Orb was spelled by the Coven. With it, you will transport to the time before the Mutari. When you arrive, you have three months to discover how to keep the dimensions intact and block Drystan's armies from invading Earth. The Densare Council believes it's possible. They asked me to send one of mine. I want you to do this. Between your skills in the field, your knowledge of spells, and the information gathered in this text, I know you can do this. I order you to accept this mission." He pushed the manuscript across his desk and extended his hand. The orb pulsed; shades of jade fire swirled within the globe.

Dad expected me to take them from his hands and follow his orders, as usual. I didn't want to touch either. Just looking at the damn green ball sent an artic wind swirling around my bones.

"When the hell do you want me to do this? We're under heavy attack, sir. You need me here. Bloody hell, you don't even know if it will work. It's a dead end," I sputtered. No way. I was not leaving. A cold sweat beaded my brow.

He sighed, placing the manuscript and orb on his desk, lowering his head and rubbing his palms across his face. With a swipe of his hands, he erased the pained expression stamped upon his face. "No one knows this, Alana. I received dispatches from the Densare Council a short time ago. Demons are attacking every compound, worldwide. We lost contact with the Council shortly after their message and I have had no luck reaching any compound. You are the counter-offensive and the only one I trust to accomplish this operation. Lieutenant, my final orders are take the orb and manuscript and go. If you do this, humanity stands a chance."

Oh gods, this was it. The one we had feared.

"How do I get back?" My voice cracked, filled with unshed tears.

"You won't." Artillery fire erupted outside the command center doors. Walls trembled as demons battered the steel.

"But … sir?" My breath strangled in my throat, fists clenched against my thighs, my nails dug gouges into my flesh … anything I could do to stifle the tears. Weakness was not acceptable in a squad leader. Deep down, I knew this was the last time I would see his face.

"Lieutenant, the troops need me. Take the orb and book. Recite the incantation." He commanded, with no hint of argument or discussion available. These were orders I must follow unquestioningly. Some, I ignored when I knew there was a better way. Yet this was not the time for disobeying a command by my superior.

My legs shook as I stood. Taking a deep, shuddering breath I raised my right hand and saluted.

"Yes sir, General." The words fell from my lips, an automated response indoctrinated in my being.

He gave me a cursory look drenched with emotion. It was more than any words of goodbye could equal. He returned my salute. "Good luck, Lieutenant."

Unable to hold myself together, tears rained unchecked down my cheeks. I did the one thing I could. I picked the manuscript and orb up off his desk. The supple leather coldly filled my left hand. The orb, a nearly weightless glass ball, felt warm in my right palm.

Steel shattered; the echoing screech reverberated in the rooms. Demons crashed through the Center door.

Chaos. My world was on fire and I knew there was nothing I could do to extinguish the flames.

Screams filled the air. The Cantati were dying. My fingers itched toward my gun.

Two enormous, gray-skinned Hatha demons, rammed the office door. Dad pushed back with his shoulder, trying to keep those brutes out of his office. He removed his Glock from its holster.

"GO, ALANA. SAY THE INCANTATION," Dad yelled. He fired into the nearest brute's hand as it curled around the door frame.

"No. Not until I know you're safe." I choked on the words. I nestled the book in my waist-band and switched the orb into my left hand. Drawing my gun from its holster with my right, I extended my arm, sighted down the barrel, and fired.

I clipped its shoulder.

"No time, Alana. Don't argue. GO," he pleaded. My gun clicked empty while the Hatha's meaty arms beat at the door.

Gasping air into my lungs, I stared into his eyes. The human world was finished and he knew it. Deep down, I felt it. As the Cantati, we were the protectors, fighting to save mankind. Our time was up. Drystan, Lord of Infernus, launched his final assault, and we failed.

Another boom from a grenade rent the air. The blast unsettled Dad's grip on the door and he faltered. The Hathas burst into the room, the demon infantry soldiers slamming him up against the remnant shards of his office door. Their razor-sharp teeth glistened in the overhead lights, a stark comparison to their dark gray skin. In the time it took me to blink, their teeth ripped into Dad.

"NO!" I screamed, loud enough that the two Hatha lifted their heads off of their current meal. They eyed me like I was a tasty morsel. These assholes were dead.

I charged. The larger one backhanded me and I crashed onto Dad's desk. My gun and the orb spilled from my fingers. I rolled out of arm's reach. The Hatha nearest to me crashed his fist onto the desk where my leg had been seconds before. Wood splintered, leaving a gaping hole in the desk. Regaining my footing, I leapt on top of the closest Hatha, removing his teeth from my father. Blood gushed from the deep hole the demon had left in Dad's shoulder. I cursed my inattention as the Hatha's arms surrounded me, cutting off my oxygen. I shoved against its mammoth jaw. This was bad. I had to help him. Dad's agonized moans filled my ears.

I swiveled my head just in time to witness the second Hatha as it ripped his body in two. "DAD!" I screamed, but no sound left my lips from my severe lack of oxygen.

Rage settled in my soul. In a single thrust, I snapped the Hatha's neck and its arms released me. I ducked low, and the second Hatha's claw grazed my arm. The screams outside Dad's office dulled as I beat the bloody hell out of it. Picking up the desk chair, I smashed it against the Hatha's skull in a single blow. Blood splattered everywhere.

I was seconds from joining the melee in the command center except I glanced in Dad's lifeless eyes.

NO.

This was not how it would end. I had to fix this. I scooped up the forgotten orb from the floor, made sure the book was still tucked in my waistband, and held the incantation. Blinking through tears, I gazed at the words scrawled upon the slip of paper.

Before another demon noticed me, I spoke, "Vicis ut est non vicis, tractus ut est non tractus, in a dies ut est non a dies. Sto procul limen inter universitas, pro ut velo ex mysterium. Possum Antiquitas Uni succurro quod servo mihi. Vicis per tractus, deleo preteritus. Ut EGO mos is, sic mote is exsisto."

The orb warmed my palm. Heat sang up my arm, encompassing my body. I couldn't move as the warmth spread.

The orb blazed fiery in my hand, so hot I wanted to drop it. Gritting my teeth through the scorching pain, my fingers dematerialized along with it. As the heat spread up my arm, I realized I couldn't move my head to check if I was missing more body parts.

And the scene before me dissolved. I'm not sure I existed anymore. It was as if I was now a void, a black nothingness. Time suspended itself. Is this what death felt like, this ceasing of all physical senses? Would it be so bad to let go into oblivion? Then my vision faltered. My eyes were open yet could see nothing.

I blinked.

My body materialized, crashing against unforgiving stone. My head thwacked against the ground as my body skidded to a halt.

Umphff, that'd leave a mark.

Blood dribbled from my chin. Each droplet connected with concrete, creating a dark puddle on the floor. I eased my shoulders and cheek off the time-worn stone. My muscles groaned, protesting the slight movement. My limbs throbbed from the jarring impact.

Through narrowed eyes, my surroundings swam into focus. I lay face-first in a gutter running along the wall. My day had turned to shit. I laughed. The sound rang sharp in the empty space.

Fuck, Dad.

Tears blurred my vision and I lay my forehead against the stone. Each breath hurt, shuddered in painful gulps into my lungs. He was dead. They all were. Raw agony gripped my heart, clenched its gnarled fist and squeezed my soul. How could they all be gone? I couldn't stifle the tears. There were not enough fingers to stop the dam.

Realization dawned as I wiped the wet trail from my cheeks. The world had ended. How the hell was I supposed to fix that?

ADDITIONAL TITLES BY TITLES BY MAGGIE MAE GALLAGHER

The Mystic Series
REMEMBER ME
CASKET GIRL

The Cantati Chronicles
RUPTURED
ANOINTED
ASCENDED

TITLES BY MAGGIE MAE GALLAGHER WRITING AS ANYA SUMMERS

The Dungeon Fantasy Club Series
HER HIGHLAND MASTER
TO MASTER AND DEFEND
TWO DOMS FOR KARA
HIS DRIVEN DOMME
HER COUNTRY MASTER
LOVE ME, MASTER ME
SUBMIT TO ME
HER WIRED DOM

The Dungeon Fantasy Club Pleasure Island Series
MASTER AND COMMANDER
HER MUSIC MASTERS

ABOUT THE AUTHOR

BORN IN ST. LOUIS, MISSOURI, Maggie grew up listening to Cardinals baseball and reading anything she could get her hands on. She remembers her mother saying if only she would read the right type of books instead binging her way through the romance aisles at the bookstore, she'd have been a doctor. While Maggie never did get that doctorate, she graduated cum laude from the University of Missouri-St. Louis with an M.A. in History.

Maggie is a bestselling and award-winning author published in multiple fiction genres. She also writes erotic romance under the name Anya Summers. A total geek at her core, when she is not writing, she adores attending the latest comic con or spending time with her family. She currently lives in the Midwest with her two furry felines.

Visit her website:

www.maggiemaegallagher.com

Visit her on social media:

Facebook: FB.me/MagMaeGallagher

Twitter: @magmaegallagher